Aliens and
Strangers

Aliens and Strangers

Sheila Jacobs

CHRISTIAN FOCUS PUBLICATIONS

© Copyright 1997 Sheila Jacobs
reprinted 2003
ISBN 1-85792-279-4
Published by
Christian Focus Publications Ltd,
Geanies House, Fearn, Tain, Ross-shire,
IV20 1TW, Scotland, Great Britain

Cover design by Alister Macinnes
Cover illustration by Graham Kennedy

Printed and bound in Great Britain by
Cox and Wyman Ltd, Reading, Berks

Contents

'All that we have accomplished you have
done for us' (Isaiah 26:12).

Aliens!

'Aliens!'

The night sky was cold and clear, but the strange, unearthly bleeping noises coming from the Galactic Scanner told of beings as yet unseen...

'They're out there.'

Bleep, bleep, bleep.

'This is it.'

Colonel Sandra Richmond stared up into the stars, her wavy auburn hair moving slightly in the cool breeze.

'Who are they? What are they?'

She wasn't frightened. She didn't know the meaning of the word 'fear'. Her diamond-shaped fighter was ready. She would zap those aliens — probably single-handed.

'What's that noise?' A sound of rushing water — louder, louder — a choking, a spluttering, a cry of frustration.

I groaned, my exciting daydream fluttering to the carpet as the noisy cistern protested again and again. Mum was trying to pull the flush.

'We'll have to get your dad to look at that toilet!' said Mum, sticking her head round my bedroom door. She switched the light on. 'Whatever are you doing here in the dark?'

'It's my room,' I said, stiffly, 'And it's not dark now!' I added, with a frown.

Mum straightened my duvet cover.

'Mum!' I exclaimed, exasperated, 'I'm busy!'

'What're you doing?'

'I'm thinking about my story.'

'Oh.'

The breeze coming through the open window had blown some of my story off the bed and onto the floor. Mum bent down and picked up one of the typewritten pages.

I snatched it away from her.

'Mum!'

'Don't forget it's school tomorrow.'

With that parting shot, she left the room. I turned the light off again, and looked out of the window.

'I don't believe it.'

I'd been waiting for this moment; waiting, hoping, watching. Now it was happening right before my eyes – and I was terrified. I backed away from the window, transfixed by the great silvery object appearing over the hill. I tried to compose myself and failed.

'Mum! Mum!'

I scrambled to the door, bumping into Mum, and grabbing at her.

'They've come! They've really come!'

'Oh, Jane, really!'

'They're out there, Mum. It's a spaceship. Ring the police or something. Quick!'

She didn't seem afraid. She leaned out of the window.

'Jane – Janie. Come and see.'

I edged up behind her and blinked into the black night. There, shining down on the garden, the meadow, and the hill beyond, was the moon.

'You've been watching too much TV,' she said, trying to sound cross, but smiling.

We looked out at the moon together.

'There's nothing to be frightened of, Janie. There aren't really any aliens coming to get you.'

'Oh, they're out there all right. I expect there'll be an inter-galactic war. Then we'll all be friends, and be able to visit them.'

'School tomorrow.'

'I wish I could visit them right now, this minute,' I muttered, as Mum shut the door behind her.

Resting my elbows on the windowsill, I watched a train rumble away in the distance, a series of lights flashing in the darkness. I wondered where the train was going. I wished I was on it.

I closed the window, and sat on my bed. The radio was still bleeping out those mysterious sounds that I half-believed were from other galaxies. I flicked the light back on and began to gather together the pages of the science fiction story I was writing. There was my heroine, Sandra Richmond, the daring, all-action space pilot, embarking on mission after mission, brave, beautiful, ambitious. All the things, in fact, that I was not, but hoped to be by the time I was grown up. After all, I was just thirteen.

Sandra Richmond! I sighed. Sandra wouldn't be scared of the moon. Sandra wouldn't be scared of anything, whereas I was frightened of everything. But then, I reasoned, Sandra didn't have to cope with school, and that scared me most.

Thinking of school tomorrow made me feel sick, as usual. The thought of St. Catherine's Girls Grammar made me groan. I hated the lessons, I was useless at games, I was scared of the teachers, and I was far from popular with the other girls. I thought of the geography homework I had dashed off that afternoon. I knew I'd get a low mark. The very thought of the geography teacher, Miss Carter, made me groan again. Careless Carter, I called her, because she always wrote 'Careless!' on my work.

I coughed. Perhaps I was going to catch a cold. I opened the window again. Maybe the night air would aggravate the condition. I coughed again. I went downstairs and coughed. It was a wasted effort – Mum wasn't downstairs.

I went back upstairs.

'Mum?'

The bathroom door was half open. The toilet was still protesting, but Mum wasn't in there. Then I saw that her bedroom light was on.

I pushed open the door, and got the shock of my life.

Mum was kneeling beside the big double bed.

She looked up when I went in. I don't know which one of us was the more embarrassed.

'Mum, what're you doing?'

'What does it look like?' she asked, sharply.

'Looks like you're praying.'

'Well – I am!'

I didn't know what to say. I'd never known Mum pray before... well, only when we stayed with Gran, and that was just at meal-times.

'What're you praying for?'

'Never you mind.' She got up, and started to make a great fuss of making the bed.

I went back into my bedroom, still feeling shocked. It was very odd. Mum didn't pray. She and Dad weren't religious. They didn't go to church. When Mum and I stayed with Gran, Mum usually made some excuse not to go to church with her. So why was she praying now?

A horrible thought hit me. Was she ill? Wasn't that the reason people prayed to God? Why else would she be praying?

I heard her starting down the stairs, and I called to her.

'Mum! Mum!'

'What *is* it, Janie?'

'Mum – you're all right, aren't you?'

There was a silence before she replied.

'Yes, I'm fine. School tomorrow, Janie. Time for bed, now.'

I wasn't entirely convinced. *Was* she ill? Or was she praying about something else? Was Gran all right? She didn't seem to telephone as much as she used to. Or maybe Mum was worried about something else.

It suddenly struck me that Dad hadn't telephoned. He always phoned on Sundays when he was away.

I tried for ages to get to sleep, but I couldn't. I waited for that comforting telephone call... it didn't come. Mum came to bed, later, and still I couldn't sleep.

I decided to try a prayer of my own. I thought it was quite likely if there was a God, he would hear me even if I wasn't kneeling... and it was *so* warm in my bed!

'Dear God,' I said, in a whisper, 'if you're out there, please look after Dad and make him ring us up.'

I felt some of the anxiety leave me, and I shut my eyes tightly.

'Also, God, please protect me from aliens.'

I fell asleep, and in the morning I discovered that God had answered one of my prayers, if not the other. Aliens hadn't zapped me in the night. But Dad hadn't telephoned, either.

St. Catherine's

Dirt and diesel and grimy windows. I tried to gaze through the grime at the blur of houses and lamp-posts. Somewhere through the greasy fog it was a sunny summer's morning.

The bus chugged past a parked car. For a minute, I thought it was my dad's. It wasn't. I wished I hadn't seen that car, because now I was worrying about Dad again. Had he had an accident? Was that why he hadn't phoned?

There was a burst of giggling from several girls in the front of the bus. They were dressed, like me, in the blue blazer and skirt of St. Catherine's. We were the only ones on the bus, apart from a few pensioners and a young woman in fashionable clothes who was trying to apply lipstick with the aid of a small hand-held mirror.

I watched her. It was incredible. She didn't get any of the lipstick on her face, just on her mouth, even though the bus lurched and bumped along. I wondered if Sandra Richmond would wear lipstick. I doubted it.

With all her space exploits and missions, she wouldn't have time to fiddle about with make-up. But if she did, I thought, as the bus slowed down, she'd put the lipstick on straight, just like that young woman, even if she was in the middle of a galactic battle. And she wouldn't be seen dead on a bus. I wished heartily that I was on a space transport ship to anywhere other than school.

'Hello!' My friend Heather had jumped on board, all glasses and big teeth.

'You look happy,' I observed.

'You know I love Mondays!' She sat next to me.

'You're mad.' I stared back through the grime, catching my own reflection, mousy-brown and tired-looking. 'Quite mad.'

'I'm not. Mum's just had a big row with Alison. Then she had a big row with Diane. It was me next, so I'm glad to get out.'

'Your mum rows with everyone.'

'Only since Dad went off with Alison.'

'How come she had a row with her just now?'

'On the phone. She found out that Alison bought Diane that make-up kit.'

'Oh!' I remembered the kit. Heather and I had tried some blue eye shadow when her sister had been out.

Heather had looked as if someone had socked her in the eye, and I was allergic to the stuff and my face swelled up.

'Alison told Diane that she was fifteen and ought to wear make-up. Mum said she looked like a tart.'

'Your mum thinks everyone – '

'She doesn't think that of you.'

'No, she thinks I'm weird.'

'Well, you are.' Heather shrugged her shoulders.

We jogged on, turning into the main road which led into town.

'How's the story going?'

'All right,' I said.

'Diane says you can't be a colonel by the time you're twenty-four.'

'Sandra Richmond is.'

'Diane says you don't get colonels that young. She says it's just not possible.'

I sat back. 'She doesn't know anything.'

'She does. She's in the "A" stream.'

And we were in the 'C' stream, the bottom stream, the dunces and lazy pupils of the school.

'Diane says there are no such things as aliens.'

'Oh yes there are!' I drew a deep breath, and stared

at my friend, wondering whether I should take her into my confidence. 'They're already here. Living amongst us.' And I felt smug as I watched her eyes go large and round.

'You've seen them?'

'I told you, they're living amongst us. There might even be one on the bus.'

Heather squirmed in her seat.

'Jane, how can you tell?'

'They're not quite human.'

Heather blinked a few times. I leaned towards her.

'Miss Carter's one.'

'What?'

'Come on, Heather. She *can't* be human. That voice is a pretty poor imitation of a human one, isn't it? And the eyes are – well, they're glassy.'

'I've never liked Miss Carter.'

'Well, there you are, then.'

Heather was interested now.

'Who else, Jane?'

'Olivia. Olivia Gates.'

'Olivia's not an alien!'

I thought about our sarcastic form captain.

'Yes she is. Have you seen the way she runs on the hockey pitch? Call that normal?' In my mind, I saw

Olivia Gates – she was very thin and very smug. Even her thin pony-tail was smug. Yuk! 'And her eyes are glassy, like Careless Carter's. Just like a robot.'

'A robot!'

'Aliens might be robots. Or androids. Part robot. Cyborgs,' I said, knowledgeably.

'Oh!' Heather looked as if she remembered something. 'When she stayed over at my house, Olivia wouldn't eat much. She says she's a vegetarian.'

'There you are!' I exclaimed, triumphantly. 'Aliens are obviously part robot and can't eat meat.'

Heather's face lit up. 'Jane! Alison's a vegetarian, too!'

'Explains a lot,' I said.

Heather's excitement had turned to fear.

'Alison's an alien!'

'She's taken over your dad's mind, and she's trying to get Diane, too. I should watch out.'

The bus jerked to a halt and all the blue uniforms started to get off.

'Aren't you scared, Jane?'

I smiled bravely. 'Of aliens? Nah! Last night – ' but I stopped. I had been going to tell Heather that I asked God for protection, but I thought better of it. I didn't mind her knowing I believed in aliens, but I didn't want her to think I prayed to God as well.

She'd think I was completely mad.

'Never mind,' I said, and we got off the bus.

I walked along behind Heather, looking at the pavement, the road, the hedge, anything, rather than raise my eyes to those familiar imposing buildings which made up the school. Then I recalled something Heather had said, and caught her arm.

'When did Olivia stay over?'

'Oh, weeks ago.'

'You didn't tell me.'

Heather bit her lip. 'Do you want to come over, tonight?'

She was trying to placate me. I frowned. I didn't like the thought of my only friend being popular with other pupils. Especially not with ones who didn't like me and weren't shy about saying so.

'OK, I'll come over.'

'Better see how much homework we get first, I suppose.'

'Oh, I'll come anyway,' I said, knowing I could slapdash anything I might have to do.

Now I had to look at the buildings. Grand, old-fashioned, well-respected, St. Catherine's was the best school in the area. That's what everyone said, anyway.

We trailed up the stairs and along the corridor. The bell had only just stopped ringing for everyone to go to their classrooms. I glanced over the balcony, down to the great hall. There was Miss Carter, stiff-backed and stern. I was glad she wasn't our form teacher this year.

'Diane says Miss Carter never got married because her fiancé was killed in the war,' said Heather.

'What war?'

'I don't know.'

'Some inter-galactic war, I expect. Probably took place in our solar system, and the spaceship crashed, and the ones that survived came to live here, in Gipley.' I turned to my friend. 'Why wasn't Diane on the bus?'

'She was crying, and she wouldn't come to school with red eyes. Mum couldn't make her. She can't make her do anything now.'

We both leaned over the balcony. A click-click of heels along the corridor made us both dart into the classroom as our form teacher came into view.

We sat next to each other in the high-ceilinged, dreary room. It was an oppressive place, with old-fashioned sash windows and rows of dusty shelves lined with ancient books. From across the room I caught Olivia's smirking glance.

'Hello, Heather!' she called.

I opened my desk, which, like the others in that room, was amongst the oldest in the school, with its pull-up top and old inkwell.

Names of pupils incarcerated before I was born were etched into the wood. I wondered if they ever managed to escape, or whether they were still wandering about the corridors, unable to get out, in some kind of time-space vacuum, trapped forever.

Mrs. Bell, our form teacher, was there now, smiling round at the class with her friendly eyes. She had the sort of grin that made you want to grin back. I liked her. She certainly wasn't an alien. She was the best teacher in the school. At least, I thought so, because she taught English, and that was about the only subject I was interested in.

'Have a good weekend, girls?'

'Yes, Mrs. Bell!' we trilled.

'So did I. I had a phone call from my daughter, in Australia.'

Australia! How come her daughter in Australia could phone, but my dad, who was only in another part of England, couldn't? I began to think about Dad again.

'Jane. Jane Collins!'

'Yes, Mrs. Bell?'

'Jane, did you hear what I said?'

'About your daughter in Australia.'

Olivia sniggered, the thin pony-tail jigging about.

'Yes, five minutes ago. Jane, you must try to apply yourself. Try a little concentration. I was telling the form that Miss Carter is not at all satisfied with the level of work being produced here. I'm sorry to say, your name is one that keeps popping up. Jane! Did you hear me? Put that desk lid down. Do you want a detention?'

I put the lid down quickly. No, I didn't want a detention! The ultimate threat. To have to stay here longer than usual? No way! How *could* Mrs. Bell have threatened me so?

'Miss Carter isn't happy with your work *or* your attitude, Jane.'

I wasn't surprised. I loathed Careless Carter, geography, maps, and I didn't care what they grew in Brazil. My carelessness had made Miss Carter complain about me, and now the one teacher whom I thought was all right was glaring at me. Sandra Richmond wouldn't take this, I thought. She'd get her cosmic ray gun out and zap Mrs. Bell, Miss Carter, the whole form – except for Heather. Heather was smiling at me, sympathetically. Her hand shot up.

'Yes, Heather?'

'Mrs. Bell, Jane's written a book.'

The class murmured. I went red.

'Is that right, Jane?'

'Mmm,' I mumbled.

'What is it about?'

'Aliens,' I half-whispered.

'What was that?'

'Aliens.'

Now the class was *giggling*. I would sort Heather out later, I decided.

'*She's* an alien!' said Olivia.

I was relieved when the door opened, and the conversation was cut short. The relief was momentary. Miss Carter was stalking into the room.

'You aren't annoyed, are you?' whispered Heather, 'I was just trying to show Mrs. Bell you aren't completely useless.'

'Thanks!' I hissed.

Mrs. Bell and Miss Carter were in a huddle by the door.

'Aliens!' I heard Olivia scoff.

I tried to close my ears to Olivia and the others who were mocking in low voices. I wanted to hear what the teachers were saying, and as I was quite close to the door, I thought I might make out a few of the words.

They were very interesting.

Miss Carter was talking; I couldn't see her face, she had her back to me, and her tone was quiet but urgent.

'Doesn't recognise me...'

I tried to look as if I wasn't listening.

'...doesn't know who I am. None of them do, as a matter of fact. Don't recognise any of us.'

Heather was listening, now, and she had caught that. We exchanged amazed glances.

Miss Carter left the room.

'Well,' said Mrs. Bell, briskly. 'Due to circumstances outside her control, Miss Carter will not be able to take you for double geography later this morning. You'll have time to read a book or do some of the homework I'm going to set you next period.'

'Great!' I grinned at Heather. She looked back at me, very impressed. 'I knew it!' I nodded, and grinned again. I knew the class was still laughing at me, but I didn't care. Miss Carter was an alien in disguise. I was right.

'You'll come over early tonight, won't you?' Heather said, 'I want to know more about –'

'I'll come as early as I can,' I promised. It was great to be popular... even if it was only with Heather.

Heather's House

'Don't rush your dinner! That's the thing with you, Janie, you rush everything and don't do anything properly.'

I began to eat deliberately slowly. Mum took a mouthful of ham salad. She pulled a face.

'Oh, Janie, don't eat that ham. Can't you taste it? It's off.'

The plate was whisked away from under my nose.

'I'll grate some cheese,' Mum said, going into the kitchen.

'I thought the ham was OK,' I called.

'It was off, Janie. It tasted awful.'

I frowned.

'That's the second time I've got ham from Welland's that was off. I'm fed up with it. It's enough to make you turn vegetarian.'

I nearly fell off my seat.

'You're not –'

'I've got some cold chicken. Fancy cold chicken, Janie?'

'Yes,' I replied, gratefully, and was much relieved to watch my mother eat the cold chicken.

'Dad will be sorry he's not here tonight. He loves cold chicken,' said Mum.

The mention of Dad made my heart flop over. I'd tried not to think of him all day.

'I don't suppose he's phoned?' I asked, as casually as I could.

Mum shook her head. I suddenly lost my appetite.

'Mum,' I said. 'You do think Dad's all right, don't you?'

'All right?' she seemed surprised. 'Why ever should he *not* be all right?'

'He didn't ring yesterday, and he usually does. That's all.'

'Of course he's all right!' Mum said, a bit too brightly.

Talking about Dad had made me think about Mum praying last night.

'I suppose Gran's all right?' I ventured.

'Yes, Gran's all right! I spoke to her last Thursday. Don't you remember? What is all this? Gran's all right, Dad's all right, I'm all right. All right?'

She wasn't all right, I thought, glumly.

After dinner, I got my bike out from the garage where I kept it when Dad didn't need to put his car in there. I waved to Mum, and pedalled away, leaving the small semi-detached houses in Willow Drive, rounding the corner, and building up speed past the hairdressers and the Co-op. I loved going fast. It was a lot like flying, I thought.

I cycled past the golf links and the primary school, and up the hill past the church. For the first time, I noticed a big board stuck outside the church building, and I stopped to read it.

'CH..CH' it read. 'What's missing?'

'UR,' I said, aloud, and smiled. I cast an eye at the list of service times. There seemed to be lots of them. My eyes rested on the words 'Sunday School' and I shuddered. Sunday School! No thanks! Five days a week were bad enough! I pedalled away.

Stopping at the church made me think about God, again. I wondered why he'd answered the prayer for protection, but he hadn't made my dad ring us up. Was my prayer faulty, somehow? I pondered, as I sped along. Perhaps God didn't like me talking to him because I'd shown so little interest in him in the past.

I'd read a book about Jesus when I was a kid, I remembered. Gran had given it to me. I wondered where that book was. Strangely, the story came back to me, quite clearly, even though it was years since I'd read the book. In it, Jesus had said something about 'ask and it will be given to you, seek and you shall find'. Well, I thought, I'd *asked* God to make my dad ring us up. I'd done my bit. God, apparently, hadn't done his.

Heather's house came into view, and I wondered whether I should have given God my name and address when I prayed. Maybe he didn't know who I was. *Should* I have given my address? Who could I ask? The thought slipped out of my mind as I propped my bike against the broken fence and pushed open the gate. Walking up the path to the front door, I couldn't fail to notice how the garden had changed over the past year. When Heather's dad had lived at home, the grass was always well cut and tidy, with finely chiselled borders. Now everything was unkempt, with weeds and grass almost up to my knees. Heather's mum's car was in the drive. It was missing a hubcap off the back right wheel.

I could hear the argument even as I rang the doorbell. Heather answered the door, wearing a resigned expression.

I went in. The argument was coming from the kitchen.

'But Mum, everyone's doing it.'

'*You're* not!'

'I am!'

'You're not!'

'You can't stop me.'

There was a crash.

'Another plate,' said Heather.

'What's happening to this family?' came the shrieking voice of Heather's mum. 'Your sister is turning into a tart, and as for you –'

Heather's brother came out of the kitchen. My jaw dropped. His usually neatly-combed collar-length brown hair was now bright yellow. He was wearing a green T-shirt, and the overall effect looked like a haystack plonked on a green field.

'Steve's dyed his hair,' Heather said, unnecessarily.

My eyes were fixed on the haystack. I didn't know whether to laugh or not. Then I realised that Steve was staring at me. He was quite good-looking – normally – and I rather liked him. He never noticed me. He was seventeen, and I was just his kid sister's friend. But now, he was actually *looking* at me.

'It's great!' I said, and he smiled at me – he smiled at *me*.

Mrs. Miller, Heather's mum, had appeared in the

doorway, and something about her troubled features reminded me of a deranged crow.

'What's happening to you, Steven? What's happening?'

'Just the image, Mum,' he replied, in a bored voice, and started up the stairs.

'Come back down here this instant! Come here. Where are you going?' demanded Mrs. Miller.

'Upstairs, Mum.'

'Don't be insolent. This is your father's doing, isn't it? Isn't it?' Mrs. Miller almost screamed. 'He's trying to drive me mad – through you! Steven! Come here!'

Steve didn't come down. Mrs. Miller turned to us, and I shrank behind my friend. My mum never got angry – well, not like this.

'And where do you think *you're* going?'

'Just up to my room, Mum, with Jane.'

I could see that Mrs. Miller was so worked up she was shaking. She said nothing more, but went back to the kitchen, and we heard her picking up the remains of the smashed crockery. Heather and I slunk upstairs to the room she shared with her sister. I was sorry to see that Diane was there, perched on her bed, a towel wrapped round her head.

'Mum saw it,' said Heather.

Diane looked up. 'Oh-oh. The alien.'

'Don't be horrible,' said Heather.

'Written any more silly rubbish lately?' Diane asked. 'Don't you know you don't get twenty-four year old colonels in – '

'You do in Space Force,' I said. 'And I *don't* write rubbish.'

'No, she doesn't,' said Heather, loyally. 'You should hear what we've found out.'

I gave Heather what I hoped was a warning glare.

'Oh, yeah. What have you found out?'

'Can't tell you,' answered Heather. 'It's a secret.'

Diane's lip curled.

'I'm going to the loo.'

I was glad to see her leave the room. Heather turned to me, eagerly.

'So what do you think, then, Jane? About Miss Carter, I mean? All that stuff about us not recognising her...'

'Like I said all along,' I replied. 'Aliens. And now we know they're among us. And she's one of them.'

'So, what now? What do we do?'

I rested my weight on one arm, and frowned.

'I don't know if Miss Carter's a vegetarian. Do you?

Do you think it's important? I mean if she *is* one, anyway, does it matter? Is being a vegetarian a sign, Jane?' Heather drew a deep breath. 'Jane, do you think they're on to you? Do you think they know you know?'

A nasty thought slipped into my mind. I tried to forget it.

'Why do you think Miss Carter had to leave school this morning? She didn't come back all day.'

'Recalled to HQ, I expect,' I said, still trying to wipe the nasty thought from my mind.

Diane came back in, then, and we both forgot all about everything except what we were seeing. Diane had taken the towel off. Her hair was yellow.

'Oh, Diane!' gasped Heather, at last.

I started to giggle. I hadn't dared laugh at Steve, but I didn't mind laughing at Diane.

'Shut up! Silly kid!' Diane snapped.

'Mum will go mad!' Heather told her, half laughing, but looking scared as well.

Diane set her mouth in a defiant line, and sat down at the dressing table. I saw a fleeting expression of horror cross her face. She tossed her hair, said, 'Looks great!' and started to brush it. Steve appeared at the door, attracted by the laughter. When he saw Diane, he doubled up, clutching the doorpost to give him some support as he roared with laughter.

'What are you laughing at? You look the same. It's your dye!' said Diane.

Steve couldn't say anything, he was laughing too hard.

'Anyway, I'm naturally fair. Well, fairish. A bit of highlight gives body and dept. Alison said so. Alison's blonde.'

'Yes, but Diane, that's not blonde.' Heather pointed out. 'That's yellow.'

'What's going on up there?'

The voice of Mrs. Miller, and her tread on the stairs, silenced the laughter. Diane stared round wildly, looking for the towel.

'It's just a joke, Mum!' Heather called.

'It's that all right!' said Steve.

'I think I should go,' I said.

Heather caught my arm, desperately. 'Don't go. She won't yell so much if you're here.'

'OK, Heather,' I said, feeling very reluctant to stay.

'Looks good. I like it!' Diane declared.

I didn't want to see any more anger. I shivered, wondering what I would do if it began to get violent. Sandra Richmond may be an expert in all sorts of defensive tactics, but I certainly wasn't.

Heather's mum was at the door, now. Steve had disappeared. Mrs. Miller's face – which I used to think quite pretty, with her big eyes, pale skin and dark hair – was now flushed, as she focused on her elder daughter.

Diane sat very still on the edge of her bed, apparently calm, but I could see her hands twisting the corner of her duvet. It was Heather who spoke first. 'Mum, Diane didn't mean to – '

Heather's mum's face suddenly lost the harassed crow look. It crumpled. She burst into tears. It was dreadful – I'd never seen an adult cry before.

'I just wanted to look grown up!' Diane shouted, jumping up. 'I'm nearly sixteen!'

'You wanted to look like *her*!'

With a huge sob, Mrs. Miller stumbled from the room.

'Now see what you've done!' Heather told Diane.

Diane was white, and her lip trembled.

'I'd better go,' I muttered.

'Yes, go. Why don't you?' Diane faced me, directing her frustration my way. 'You're always here. Haven't you got a home to go to?'

'Oh, don't go!' Heather pleaded.

'Yes, I must. My dad's phoning tonight. I want to be there.' Unfortunately, this was the worst thing I could have said.

'Oh, your *dad's* phoning! And where is Daddy? Away again? He's always away, isn't he?' Diane spat.

'He's working,' I said, backing to the door.

'Oh, yeah!'

'In London.'

'London? Are you sure?'

'Of course I'm sure. What do you mean?'

'How come he's never at home?'

'I told you. He's working. He comes home most weekends, if he can. But it's too far to travel – '

'Oh, yeah? Looked at a map recently? London's not *that* far, you know!'

'Don't, Di,' said Heather. 'You're being horrible.'

'No I'm not. Just facing facts.'

'What facts?' I asked, in a small voice.

'He's got an Alison.'

I tried to say something, but the words wouldn't come.

'Did you hear me, alien? He's got a woman, I bet. Listen, when our dad met Alison *he* stayed away for ages. I expect your parents will get a divorce.'

'No they won't!' I felt a great surge of hate for Diane, mingled with panic at the thought of a divorce.

Diane shrugged her shoulders, and turned away. I almost ran down the stairs, just wanting to get out.

I didn't even say goodbye to Heather.

I cycled home as fast as I could go. My head was whirring with all the terrible things Diane had said. I'd been having some nasty ideas about my dad even before she had said anything, but now it was far worse. It had crossed my mind that it was likely that aliens were trying to split up families on earth; at least, it looked that way if Alison was one of them. Then I'd thought about my missing dad and Miss Carter's sudden departure from the school. Had she got my dad somewhere, held hostage? But as I raced home, I knew with a sudden feeling of sheer terror, I'd rather have aliens capture my dad than have my parents divorce.

What if it was true? What if Dad *did* have someone else? Would Mum turn into a shrieking, miserable Mrs. Miller? How would we live? Would I ever see my dad again? Would I want to? As I reached home, I wished something I had never wished before. I wished with all my heart that I had an elder brother or sister (a nice one, not like Diane) to talk to.

I shoved my bike in the garage, and pushed the back door open. I could hear the TV in the living room.

'You're home early!' commented Mum.

She seemed quite happy. She wasn't praying.

Perhaps that was what she had been praying about...
Dad's Alison.

'And before you ask, no, your dad hasn't phoned.'

'I've got some homework.' I headed out of the room,
to my bedroom. I shut the door, threw myself on the
bed, and started to cry. 'Oh God. Why don't you just
make him ring? Don't let it be true. Just make him ring.'

Miss Carter turned on the light and shone it down
on the small town of Gipley. It was a pretty town,
nestling in the Cotswolds, yes, a pretty town...

'About twenty thousand inhabitants.'

'It will be easy,' said the silver-suited alien, with
the pony-tail. 'Shall we zap them now, before taking
over Britain?'

'No. Where is the prisoner?'

'With Alison.'

'I'll get my revenge!' declared Miss Carter, icily,
'I'll get my revenge on the country of Great Britain,
and this world, for the death of Zoggo, my fiancé!'
Her voice broke a little. 'Smashed to pieces on the
M4! Two lorries and a fuel tanker; what chance did
his little spaceship have? Run over. Flat! How was
he to know it was a motorway? How could he have

known?' She leaned on the control panel, her knuckles whitening. 'I saw it all...' She sighed. 'Yes, Olivia, I saw it all.'

Just then, the door of the command centre was kicked in. There stood —

'Sandra Richmond! Oh no!'

'Oh yes!' cried Sandra, levelling her cosmic ray gun at Miss Carter. 'It's over, alien. I've zapped Alison, and the prisoner Mr. Collins is free.'

Zap! Miss Carter disintegrated in a shower of sparks. So did the pony-tailed alien, with a last cry of, 'She's an alien!'

'Sandra, are you all right?' came the deep voice of Colonel Paul Sinclaire, Sandra's colleague. Tall, handsome, brave and noble, he was madly in love with Sandra.

'I'm fine,' said Sandra. 'Just great. We've zapped them all. The world is safe.'

'Thanks to you, Sandra,' said Paul.

'Oh, yes, well. It was nothing.' Sandra looked at him. 'I really like the new hair colour, Paul. Yellow really suits you.'

There was a sudden noise; a familiar noise. And a voice.

'Jane. Jane!'

I tumbled off the bed, rubbing my eyes. I'd cried myself to sleep!

'What is it, Mum?' I shouted.

'Didn't you hear the phone? It's your dad. He wants a word with you.'

Twenty minutes later, I crawled into bed, feeling a totally different person. Everything was all right, after all. Dad had just been ill with a stomach upset, and unable to ring us the night before. He said he'd eaten some pork which was off. I dismissed any thoughts about aliens and meat as I switched off my bedside lamp, and smiled into the darkness.

Just before I turned over to go to sleep, a thought hit me. With all the excitement, I hadn't realised. God had answered my prayer. I snuggled down, and shut my eyes. Dad had telephoned. He'd only had a little stomach upset. No big deal – no Alisons. Dad had rung. It was all OK.

I opened my eyes again. He *was* away a lot. Why was he? Nobody else's dad worked such long hours. Nobody else's dad was away from home so much.

Well, mine was, and that was that. Closing my eyes again, I drifted off to sleep. And I'm sorry to say that I forgot to thank God for answering my prayer.

Dad, God and Spacemen

'That's Diane!'

I stepped back a few paces and stopped, pretending to study a picture on the hairdresser's door. But I wasn't really looking at it. I was staring past, into the salon. Yes, it was Diane. She had seen me. So had the lady who owned the shop, and who was waving me away from the door. A girl was busy soaping Diane's hair. I started to laugh. Diane glared at me, and looked as if she would like to thump me. But she couldn't, she was trapped, her neck bent backwards over the sink.

The lady who owned the shop tapped her scarlet fingernails on the window and mouthed, 'Go away!' and I did, still giggling. It was the first time that day I had felt happy.

My school bag was heavy with books. I had lots of homework. It had been a very lonely day. Olivia Gates had not been at school, which was nice, and neither had Diane – but Heather had been missing, too.

After the events at Heather's house the previous evening, I wondered whether my friend had joined the Yellow Hair Club, and that was why she hadn't been at school. I would telephone her later and find out.

I rounded the corner and got my first glimpse of home. My heart leapt. There, in the driveway, was a big silver car.

'Dad!'

I began to run, squeezing past Dad's car and almost falling into a rose bush. I stumbled through the back door.

'Dad! Dad!' He was in the living room, sitting on the sofa, a plate of sandwiches balancing on his knee.

'Dad!'

'Good grief!' he said, 'What a welcome!'

I slung my school bag down. It knocked into a small table, and a vase of flowers fell to the carpet.

'Jane! Steady!' Dad's voice was muffled, because I was hugging him.

'What happened to my flowers?' asked Mum, coming into the living room. 'Oh, Janie!'

Never mind any silly flowers! I thought. Dad's home!

'Janie – Janie! Watch Dad's sandwiches!'

'Dad, I've really missed you!'

'Yes, so I gathered,' said Dad.

I sat back. I'd squashed his sandwiches, but he didn't seem to mind.

'How are you, Dad?'

'I'm all right, Jane. How's school, sweetheart?'

'School's school.'

'Oh. I see.'

Mum was mopping up the water, and putting the flowers back in the vase. Dad looked at me, and glanced at Mum. I knew what he meant.

'I'm sorry about the flowers, Mum.'

Dad took a bite from one of his flattened sandwiches.

'So you're all right, then?' I said.

'Jane, what is this? I must say, I don't usually get such a warm – ' Dad swallowed hard. 'Nothing wrong, is there? I mean, you haven't done anything terrible, have you?'

'Of course not!'

'Then why – '

'Janie's just been a bit worried about you,' Mum told him. 'It was because you didn't phone when you usually do.'

I didn't know whether to point out that *she'd* been worried, too. In fact, she'd been so worried about something (and I was sure it was Dad) that she'd been praying. So had I, of course. Should I mention this to Dad? I was thinking about it when he said,

'Oh yes, before I forget – Gran says "hello".'

'You've seen Gran!'

'Yes. Just popped in on the way back from – '

'Is she all right?'

Dad blinked a bit. 'Yes, she's fine. Jane – '

'She's been worried about Gran, too,' said Mum.

Dad put his arm round me.

'Well, there's no need to worry about me, and there's certainly no need to worry about your gran. She was having a little party when I turned up.'

'A party?' I repeated.

'Yes, sort of. Some of her weird friends were there. You know, the ones we try to avoid when we visit.'

'Oh!'

'They were having some sort of Bible meeting. Luckily I came in at the end, just in time for coffee and biscuits. There were some strange characters there, Jane. I thought one of the old dears was dead until she said she wanted to go to the toilet.'

'Speaking of toilets – ' said Mum.

'Another one of them – ancient, very intense, with beedy little eyes – asked me if I "believed". I said I believed in football, cricket and that God was a Spaceman. I don't think she knew what to say!'

I don't think we did, either. Mum suddenly looked embarrassed. I was shocked, and only partly relieved when Dad leaned back and began to laugh so heartily that I knew it was a joke.

I thought I'd better make sure.

'You don't, do you, Dad?'

'Don't what, Jane?'

'Don't believe God was a Spaceman?'

Dad laughed again, but I noticed that he didn't give me a direct answer.

Shortly afterwards, I went upstairs to do some serious thinking. I was overjoyed that Dad was back, but his remark about God being a Spaceman had made me feel uncomfortable. I sat on my bed, fingering the scattered pages of my story. The uncomfortable feeling got stronger.

I went to the open window, and looked out.

God was a Spaceman! I heard my dad say it in my mind. Again, the uncomfortable feeling. All of a sudden, I knew why I felt like that.

'God!' I whispered out of the window. 'God, listen. Dad was only joking about you being a Spaceman. At least, I think he was joking. Anyway, whether he was or not – I don't believe you were – or are – a Spaceman.'

The uncomfortable feeling disappeared. 'Oh yes,' I said, 'And I forgot to say thanks for getting my dad to ring us. And you even made him come home when we weren't expecting him. That's great. I do believe in you, God. Yes, I do.'

I felt excited. It was as if I'd made contact with a new friend. It was comforting to know that he was there – and I knew beyond doubt that he was.

I didn't have long to think about God. I had to do history homework. After struggling for half an hour with Roman Britain, and flipping through a chapter of some dreary book we were reading for English, I heard the doorbell ring.

'Jane! It's Heather.'

Minutes later, Heather was in my room, looking through my homework. I was glad to see her hair wasn't yellow.

'You didn't miss much,' I said. 'I hope you're going to be at school tomorrow.'

'Yes.' She frowned. 'You've got this wrong. The Romans didn't invent the first TV.'

'They might have done. There's a lot we don't know!'

'There's a lot *you* don't know,' said Heather, goggling at what I'd written. 'This essay is rubbish, Jane.'

'You can do it, if you like.'

Obligingly, she did do it.

'Do you want to stay for tea?' I asked, very grateful.

'No, I can't. Mum doesn't even know I've slipped out. Oh – is this your book? Can I read it?'

'Well – ' She read the last paragraph out loud.

'"Well done, Sandra. You've saved the earth!" said the Supreme Commander.

"It was nothing," Sandra said, modestly, "I did have some help from the rest of Space Force."

"It's not over, though." The Supreme Commander shook his head. "They won't give up that easily. They're planning something. Something really big."

"Not too big for Sandra to handle!" said Paul Sinclaire.

"Have a good weekend. See you Monday!" said the Supreme Commander, and switched the office lights off.'

Heather looked at me. 'Jane, you can't tell me that Space Force doesn't work weekends?'

'What?'

'Jane, if the aliens attacked on Saturday, or Sunday -'

'Who's writing this story?'

She shrugged her shoulders, and put down the pages.

'Anyway,' I said, 'That last bit you just read – it's based on truth.'

'Is it?'

'Yes. There's something going on, all right. Miss Carter was back at school today, but Olivia was off.'

'So? I was off, too, remember?'

'Yes, but Heather, don't you see? One of them has to be at the controls of their spaceship while the others are pretending to live ordinary lives. The ship is probably hidden somewhere near Gipley. Maybe in the woods.'

'Wouldn't it have hit the trees – '

'Or it could be in orbit round the earth.'

Heather bit her lip.

'I haven't thought much about aliens today,' she confessed.

'Anyway, where were you? You don't look ill.'

'I didn't sleep much last night. It was awful. Mum was so upset.' She sighed, and I made a mental note that it might be useful to remember a good night's sleep was essential for schooling. I wondered how I could manage to stay awake one night, and present myself looking tired and useless the next morning. Mum would surely send me back to bed. It was worth a try.

'I saw Diane in the hairdressers,' I said.

'Yes, she's having her hair sorted out, and she's promised Mum that she'll go back to school tomorrow. I'm sorry about what she said to you about your dad.'

'It's OK.' And it was – I was confident about my parents' marriage now that Dad was home again. 'Dad's back. Didn't you see his car?'

'Yes.'

'He's been working very hard, and he's been ill as well. And he's been to see my gran.'

'Do you get to see your gran much?'

'No,' I said, sadly, remembering my gran's kindly face and bright eyes. I loved her very much. She was tall and thin and very funny. 'She lives miles away – in Essex.'

'You've only got one gran, haven't you? So have I – Nanna Miller. I don't see her much, either, although she lives in Gipley.'

'How come you don't see her, then?'

'Oh, she lives in a Home with lots of other old people.'

'Does that mean you can't visit her?'

'No – ' Heather's eyes lit up. 'Jane! Why don't we go and see Nanna Miller?'

'What, you and me?'

'Yes. I haven't seen Nanna for ages and ages. Mum

51

won't take us to see her any more – not since Dad moved in with Alison.'

I frowned.

'Mum hates all Dad's side of the family, now,' Heather explained, 'But I don't see why I shouldn't go and see Nanna, just because she's my *dad's* mum. I mean, she's still my nanna.'

'You mean you're not going to tell your mum?'

'About our visit? No.'

I thought of the harassed crow.

'Don't you think she'll be angry if she finds out?'

'It'll be OK. She won't find out.' Heather had a far-away expression on her face. 'You'll love Nanna, Jane. She's round and fat and she's got rosy cheeks, just like two apples. Oh yes, Jane. Let's go and see Nanna. Let's go on Saturday!'

It seemed a daring thing to do – visit without permission. I didn't really understand why Mrs. Miller had stopped Heather visiting her nanna. It didn't seem fair. In fact, it was odd. I didn't say anything, but something about the situation seemed distinctly alien. It would be an interesting trip.

'You're definitely going to be at school tomorrow, aren't you, Heather? It's double geography. You know I hate Wednesdays.'

Mum was shouting up the stairs. 'Jane! Jane! Didn't you hear the phone? Are you going deaf? It's Heather's mother.'

Fear flashed across Heather's features. 'Mrs. Collins, can you tell Mum I'm on my way home?'

'I think she wants to speak to you!' called Mum.

Heather rolled her eyes, and we went downstairs. Mum handed the telephone receiver to Heather, who looked guilty.

A firm grip on my arm yanked me into the living room, and Mum shut the door so that Heather could have some privacy.

'Mrs. Miller is furious. She didn't even know Heather was out until she called her for tea!'

'Oh.'

Heather came into the living room, very red.

'Does Heather want a lift home?' asked Dad, getting up.

'No thanks, Mr. Collins. It's OK. I'll walk.'

'I'll come with you,' I said, and Mum nodded her approval.

Heather's face was still like a red football as we walked down the road together.

'You're so lucky, Jane. Your dad is really nice.'

'Your dad is nice, too.'

'Yes, but he's not nice to Mum.'

We walked on, and Heather began to sniff.

'Come on, Heather. It'll be all right.'

'You know, Jane, I'm really looking forward to seeing Nanna. I was always her favourite. She told me so.'

A car stopped across the road. I knew the car. It had a missing hubcap.

'Heather! Get in!'

Mrs. Miller didn't acknowledge me at all. Heather got into the car, and didn't even have time to wave before it pulled away, tyres screeching on the dry road. I wondered if Mrs. Miller had always driven so fast. I didn't think so.

I was standing on the kerb with no reason to be anywhere but home, so I turned round and started back. It was a sunny evening, and the gardens on our estate were full of red, yellow and white flowers. The only problem with mid-summer was the end of term exams which were coming up. Still, once those were out of the way, it would be the summer holidays. Weeks and weeks with no school.

Wonderful!

With these happy thoughts, I ambled up the drive, pushing past Dad's car and getting a face full of rose bush. It was then that I heard the noise.

Raised voices.

Yes, it was. Raised voices.

I felt cold, even on that warm evening.

The back door was open, and I could hear them. It was Mum and Dad. They were arguing. It wasn't just an argument. It was a row. I'd never heard them really row before.

I walked into the kitchen.

'Oh – hello, sweetheart!' said my dad, lamely.

Mum brushed her hair back with her hand, and carried on cooking the dinner as if nothing had happened. But her cheeks were flushed.

'Will you get my washing in, Janie?' Mum asked, in a very even voice.

I did as I was asked. I couldn't stop my hand from shaking as I took the washing off the line. All the fears that had gone when I saw that my dad was home, came flooding back. Something was wrong.

And as I stood in the garden, clutching the washing, I looked round at the house and realised that I didn't want to go back in.

Trouble!

Maps, maps, maps. Maps of South America. Maps of Africa. A big map of Great Britain. And the globe itself, dangling by a wire from the ceiling. It was quiet. Very quiet. Too quiet, thought Sandra Richmond. A cruel laugh pierced the silence.

'Careless Carter!'

'Surprised, Colonel Richmond? Yes, I expect you are!' Miss Carter emerged from the shadowy recesses of the room. She ripped open her floral jacket to reveal a slightly burnt silver suit.

'You don't get rid of us quite so easily!'

Sandra could smell charred space suit.

'Where am I? How did I get here?'

'I'll get my revenge. Yes, I'll be avenged for Zoggo's death. My beloved Zoggo! Do you hear me, Colonel Richmond? Do you hear me?'

'Yes, I hear you.'

'Do you think we don't know all about you? All about your town, your country, your world? Do you think I don't know what shape Brazil is?'

'What?'

'Brazil. I couldn't recognise it.'

'Well, you were quite high up, weren't you? In the spaceship?'

'I beg your pardon?'

'In the — '

'Jane Collins! I've had just about enough of you!'

I sat bolt upright. 'I'm sorry, Miss Carter!'

'What's the matter with you? You look half asleep!'

Half asleep? I'd been fully asleep!

'Jane's not feeling very well today, Miss Carter,' piped up Heather, 'Perhaps she's got what I had yesterday.'

'Hmm. Well, it doesn't excuse that map.'

Miss Carter slapped the exercise book down on my desk. My hurried homework had 'Careless!' written beside the very wobbly map of Brazil.

'Do it again.'

'Yes, Miss Carter.'

'If I don't see an improvement in your standard of work soon, Jane, you'll have a detention.'

The bell sounded for the end of the lesson – and the end of afternoon school.

'Homework!' rasped Miss Carter, 'I would remind you all that the end of term exams aren't far away, so I hope you are revising. In addition to revision, read chapter thirty in your red books, please – "Exports and Food Production".'

'Nuts, Miss Carter,' said Heather.

'I beg your – '

'Brazil nuts, Miss Carter. We eat them at Christmas.'

We filed out of the classroom.

'That was a brave attempt to draw her out!' I said.

'What do you mean?'

'Trying to find out if she has a reaction to food... pity you couldn't have mentioned some sort of meat. Corned beef! You could have said corned beef. Or is that Argentina?'

'I don't know what you're talking about. I like Brazil nuts.'

'I'll tell you what's nuts, Heather!' lisped a voice behind us. 'Jane is nuts! She was asleep in that lesson.'

'Can you think of anything better to do in geography?' I snapped.

Olivia Gates smirked. 'Got to do your map again, Jane? What a shame!'

I watched Olivia trot away, thin pony-tail bouncing.

'Come on, Jane. You don't look well at all. It's a good job we've got a lift home tonight,' said Heather.

I was so tired. I had hardly slept the night before, and it wasn't something I had deliberately engineered to get time off school. I was so worried about Mum and Dad. There had been a terrible atmosphere at home after they had had their argument. They both tried to appear happy, but I knew they were pretending. And I knew Mum wasn't her usual self when I complained that morning that I hadn't slept. Instead of looking sympathetic and fussing over me, she just packed me off to school.

I'd held out for as long as I could but geography, last lesson on a hot afternoon, had finished me off.

'It's nice of your dad to give us a lift home,' Heather said. 'Diane was really jealous when I said I wouldn't be catching the bus.'

We had arrived at the school gates. There were several cars waiting, but Dad's wasn't there yet.

'It's OK,' Heather chattered. 'He'll be along in a minute. We don't mind waiting, do we, Jane? Diane would have killed for a lift home. She hates her hair, you know. That's why she was so quiet on the bus this morning. Horrible, isn't it? A kind of sick mouse colour. They had to dye it – Jane? Are you awake?'

'Yes.' I leaned against the gate post.

'I'm so looking forward to Saturday, Jane. We're going to have a wonderful time. Just the thought of seeing Nanna again has really cheered me up. I've been feeling a bit – '

'Heather,' I said. 'Can you keep a secret?' She nodded, wide-eyed. 'Aliens. They're after *my* family, now.'

'Oh, Jane!'

'It's not a game any more.' Even as I said it, in such a battle-hardened tone, I felt like Sandra Richmond herself.

'But how do you know?'

'Can't say.'

A car drew up.

'What are you waiting for? Get in!' barked Mrs. Miller, as the passenger doors were flung open.

'Mum?'

'Heather, get in. You too, Jane.'

'What's going on?' Heather asked, as we climbed into Mrs. Miller's car. 'We weren't expecting you, Mum.'

'No, I know that. Jane's mother telephoned me and said Jane's father couldn't pick you up after all.'

'We could have caught the bus if we'd known,' said Heather, 'Then you wouldn't have had to – '

'Yes, you could have done, if the telephone call hadn't come out of the blue twenty minutes ago!'

I sank down in the back seat. I didn't know what to say. I could see Mrs. Miller's crow-like stare as she glared at me from the rear-view mirror.

'I'd only just got in from work!' she said. 'It's a pity your mother doesn't drive, Jane!'

I sighed, wondering why my dad had not been able to pick us up. Surely he wasn't ill again? Why did Mum leave it to the last minute to telephone Mrs. Miller? A cold knot appeared in my stomach.

We pulled up at traffic lights. Mrs. Miller eyed me from the mirror.

'Are you all right, Jane?'

'She's not feeling well, Mum.'

'Not going to be sick, are you?'

'No, Mrs. Miller.'

We drove on. She kept glancing at me in the mirror. I wondered how she could keep an eye on me and drive at the same time. It didn't seem possible. In fact, it seemed unearthly.

Mrs. Miller is definitely an alien, I thought. Look at those eyes... she's probably more used to flying a spaceship through asteroid belts than driving through traffic in Gipley.

The next thing I knew, someone was calling my name. I woke up with a start. We'd stopped. I was home.

Heather and her mother were peering over the back of their seats.

'My goodness, Jane!' exclaimed Mrs. Miller. 'You didn't have games or swimming today, did you?'

'No,' I mumbled. 'Geography.'

I almost fell out of the car. Muttering, 'Thanks!' I tottered up the drive. It occurred to me that I didn't have a face full of rose bush like I normally did when Dad's car was in the drive. Then I realised, I wasn't having to squeeze past a car at all.

Our driveway was empty. I pushed open the back door.

'Mum?'

'In here, Janie,' said her voice from the living room.

She was doing the ironing. The television was on. There was no sign of Dad.

'Why didn't Dad pick us up?'

'Dad's not here.'

'Why not?'

'He's gone back to work.'

My heart flipped over.

'He was only on a flying visit.' Mum wiped her forehead with the back of her hand. 'He only popped home because he couldn't get back any other time. He's been very busy.'

'But why did he say he'd pick us up if he knew he'd be going back to work?'

She sighed, heavily. 'Because he didn't know he'd have to go back so soon. He hoped to be here another day or so.'

'But why – '

'Oh Janie, please! It's too hot for questions.'

I stood there, feeling stubborn.

'I heard you arguing yesterday.'

Mum started ironing one of my blouses.

'Mum, I said – '

'I know.'

'What were you arguing about, Mum? Was it – '

'Oh, Janie! *Everybody* argues!'

'But – '

'That's enough!' She slammed the iron down. 'I've got enough to think about without you going on and on. Go and do your homework. Leave me in peace! Go on – leave me alone!'

I shot upstairs as if someone had strapped fireworks to my backside. Mum had never ever told me to leave her alone before. What was happening? The world was falling apart. Too tired, too upset to even think about my homework, I chucked my school bag onto the bed, and paced around until the smell of bacon and sausages wafted into my room, accompanied by a little knock-knock, as Mum's head appeared round the door.

'Coming down for tea, Janie?'

'Don't know,' I said, miserably.

'Aren't you hungry?'

I was starving, but I said, 'Don't know.'

'There's good telly tonight.'

'Got to do my homework.'

'Haven't you done it? You've been up here for ages.'

I looked at her. I could see that she was trying to be cheerful, but it was the same kind of forced happiness as I'd seen yesterday.

'You don't look very well,' said Mum.

'I don't *feel* very well.'

'Oh dear. I hope it's not a bug.'

I shrugged my shoulders.

'Maybe you should go to bed early tonight, and we'll see how you are in the morning.'

I nodded. I was sure I'd feel awful in the morning. Just awful enough not to go to school.

Later, I was in bed, homework still undone (well, I wouldn't need it tomorrow, would I?), a cup of cocoa on the bedside table, and Mum leaving the room after having made a fuss of me. I was feeling better already. A day off school would help me get my thoughts together, I told myself. Aliens! There were more of them around than I'd realised at first. Their mission appeared to be breaking up families, and taking over family members... oh yes, and infiltrating schools.

I reached for the typewritten pages of my story. I found the paragraph where I had described Sandra Richmond's parents. With a few strokes of my biro, I made her an orphan. I thought it was safer for her.

But that didn't help *me*. I wasn't an orphan. I'd seen what had happened to Heather's family, and now something sinister was happening to mine. I had to face it; something was definitely wrong between my mum and dad. But what did you do when you were faced with a situation like this? What did you do when your parents argued and your dad spent more and more time away from home?

I slipped out of bed, and padded over to my book shelf. Searching for the right title, I found the book I wanted. It was about alien sightings and UFO encounters. But as I leafed through it, I could find nothing that gave any advice about what to do when you suspected alien influences on your own family.

I rifled through some of my other books. I had several about all sorts of eerie happenings and frightening events – but none could tell me what to do or where to go for help when you were scared.

'What are you meant to do?' I murmured. 'Who can I ask?'

A little book that had been dislodged by my rummaging suddenly fell onto the carpet. I bent down and picked it up. To my astonishment, it was the little book about Jesus that I had read when I was a kid.

I looked at the brightly coloured cover. I thought I'd lost this book ages ago. It was actually called, *What Did Jesus Say?* and I started to flip through it, rather disdainfully at first – after all, this book was for little kids. There was a saying of Jesus on the left hand page, and pictures on the right. One picture that caught my eye was of a man in a long white robe. He had collar-length brown hair, and his hand was lifted up as he taught a crowd of people. I stared at the face and wondered whether Jesus had really looked like that and how the person who drew the picture would know.

Opposite the picture were the words I'd remembered about asking and receiving. Well, I thought – I *had* received. God had answered my prayer.

Dad had phoned, and had even come home. Trouble was, he had gone again.

I got back into bed, clutching the little book. 'Does God want me to pray *again*?' I pondered out loud. I turned over a couple of pages. Another saying of Jesus caught my eye: *'Do not worry about tomorrow, for tomorrow will worry about itself.'*

I looked through the rest of the book, reading what Jesus taught the people of long ago, but I kept coming back to that piece 'Do not worry...' and I wondered if God was trying to tell me something.

I put the book down, and shut my eyes, clasping my hands together like I thought you should when you prayed properly.

'Dear God,' I began, in a whisper, and 'it's me again.' I thought quickly, and added, 'Jane Collins, 10 Willow Drive, Gipley, Gloucestershire. I talked to you before about my dad and also about the aliens. And I said that I didn't believe you were a Spaceman. Do you remember? Well, bad news, God. My dad's gone back to work, and my mum's not happy, even though she's putting on a brave face. And they were rowing yesterday.' I clasped my hands together even tighter. 'Your Son Jesus said we shouldn't worry, but I am worried, God. Really worried.'

A Weird Visit

'I don't know how you do it.'

'Do what?'

Heather fingered the bunch of roses she was carrying, and looked sideways at me.

'You know. Get the rest of the week off school, just because you felt a bit ill on Wednesday.'

I didn't reply. Two days at home feeling 'under the weather' had agreed with me. Mum seemed happier, too – and she wasn't pretending. I thought it had something to do with Dad telephoning every evening, which he didn't usually do when he was away.

I'd tried to forget all my fears, convincing myself that everything was all right really. Any lingering doubts – along with uneasy feelings because I had done so little revision and the exams were only days away – were pushed firmly to the back of my mind that afternoon.

'Do these smell enough?' Heather shoved the roses under my nose.

'What do you mean, smell enough? They smell like roses normally smell.'

'Jane.' Heather turned to me, her face suddenly anxious. 'I am doing the right thing, aren't I?'

'You want to visit your nanna, don't you? Well – that's what you're doing!'

'Yes, but Jane, I had to lie to my mum. I said we were going shopping.' Heather bit her lip. 'Did you tell your mum we were going shopping?'

'No, I said we were going into town.'

Heather bit her lip again. I felt quite clever – after all, I hadn't actually lied to Mum. Feeling smug was very satisfying. I could see why Olivia Gates made an almost constant habit of it.

'Oh, don't worry,' I said. 'Just think how thrilled your nanna will be when she sees you.'

Heather cheered up straight away.

'You're right, Jane. Come on. Let's cross over – that's the Home, over there.'

We walked across the road, and up to a big white five-barred gate. There was a notice attached to it. It said: 'Hollytrees Home for the Elderly'. I looked at the large grounds. There were lots of trees – fir trees, an old oak, and some young willows – but I couldn't see any holly trees. I was about to point this out, but my friend was already crunching up the gravel drive.

'Come on, Jane.'

It was like a park, and we didn't actually see the Home itself until we were half way up the drive. The drive swung round to the right, and we swung round with it, and there in front of us, totally shielded from the road by all the trees, was something that made me shiver.

'It's nice, isn't it!' Heather said, brightly. 'I bet it used to be a mansion. I bet a millionaire used to live here.'

I bet it was a prison, I thought. It looked horrible. My eyes travelled over the grey walls, and what seemed to be hundreds of windows. It reminded me of school.

I didn't want to go in.

'Let's have a look round, first,' I suggested.

Rather reluctantly, Heather followed me around the side of the old building. There were a few broken down sheds, and a tall fence. There was a gate, but it wouldn't open.

We walked beside the fence until we found a place where one of the wooden slats was missing. Peering through, we could see lawns, a pond, bushes and more trees. We could also see a paved area with seats. Some of the old folk were sitting there, lined up, facing the pond. We watched them. They didn't talk. They didn't move.

'Do you think they're all right?' asked Heather, in a low voice.

'Don't know.'

'They don't look all right, do they?'

'They look as if they're in another world...'

'Odd.'

'Very odd!' There was something alien going on here, I thought. 'Heather – '

'Can we go in, now? I want to see Nanna.'

'OK.'

We went round to the front door. It had a very strange handle. It was high up, and had to be manipulated with a lower handle.

'It must be to stop them escaping!' I muttered.

Certainly there was something menacing about the place. Once we had opened the door, and stepped into the dark hall, I had a nasty feeling that we might never get out again.

There was a smell of polish. It was a familiar smell – it must have been the same kind of polish they used at school. I shuddered.

A glass door straight ahead led into some sort of lounge area. I peered through the glass.

Two old ladies, one leaning heavily on a stick, stared back at me. It was a weird sensation – like one of us was in a zoo and the other was observing the exhibit. Trouble was, I wasn't sure which of us was which.

'Can I help you?'

A kind-faced woman was in the hall now, smiling. She was dressed all in white, and she was wearing a badge with 'Hilary' written on it.

'I've come to visit my nan – I mean, my grandmother,' said Heather.

'What's her name?'

'Mrs. Miller.'

Hilary smiled again and nodded. 'Yes, she's in the lounge.'

She pushed open the glass door, and we went in. The two old ladies were still staring. Apart from them, and an old man who was slumped in a very uncomfortable-looking plastic chair, there was only a thin-faced bundle of bones, wrapped up in a purple cardigan, fast asleep in another chair, her mouth hanging open in a small 'o'.

'No.' Heather shook her head. 'She's not here.'

Hilary looked puzzled.

'Yes she is, look, over there – asleep.'

Heather's eyes almost popped out of her head.

'Oh, no. That's not my nanna. My nanna is much younger, and fatter – no, that's not her.'

'This is the only Mrs. Miller we have,' said Hilary, gently, 'Kathleen Miller.'

'Oh!' Heather's hand shot to her mouth.

'What's up?' I asked.

'Oh – it *is* her!'

Hilary was obviously becoming concerned about us. She followed us over to the old lady who was fast asleep. 'Kath – Kath!' Hilary touched the purple cardigan. 'Someone to see you.'

The old lady woke up, blinking with faded blue eyes, her white face very lined and shrunken. She had no teeth.

'Kath – look who's here,' said Hilary.

'It's me, Nanna. Heather.'

The faded eyes rested on Heather.

'Heather?'

'Yes, Nanna.'

I nudged my friend. She had been holding the bunch of roses so tightly that the paper was crumpled. She gave the flowers to her grandmother.

'These are for you, Nanna.'

'For me?' said Nanna Miller, and she really did look delighted.

Heather's voice was slightly trembly as she spoke again. 'How are you, Nanna?'

'Who did you say you were?' Nanna Miller asked.

'I'm Heather.'

'Heather?'

'Your – your granddaughter. Don't you remember, Nanna?'

'Granddaughter?'

'Yes, Nanna.' Heather was fighting back tears now. 'There's me, and Diane, too. And your grandson, Steve.'

'Steve? My son is Tom.'

'Yes, Nanna. But your *grandson* is Steve.'

'Tom.' The old lady half rose out of her chair. 'I've got to be getting home, now. I've got to look after Tom. He's only six, and he's been so poorly. I've got to go home.'

'Come on, now, Kath!' Hilary put an arm round Nanna Miller, and then she glanced at Heather. 'Are you all right?'

'No,' said Heather, in a small voice.

'Go into the office and I'll bring you both some tea. Then we can have a little chat. Look – it's just down the hall, and on the left. I'll be with you in a minute.'

'I feel sick,' said Heather.

Hilary frowned. 'Surely you know that your nanna gets a bit forgetful?'

Heather turned round and fled from the lounge. I went after her.

'Wait, Heather. Wait!'

Heather was trying to get out of the front door. She didn't remember about the handle, but I did. The next moment we were both outside, and she was leaning against the hot stone wall, her eyes dry now, and too bright.

'Heather? Are you OK?'

She didn't answer me.

'Heather? You look really strange. Perhaps we should have that tea.'

'No.'

'Heather – '

'I don't want to talk about it. I don't want to talk about it!'

She shot off down the gravel drive, and I ran to catch up with her.

'Heather! Look out – there's a car!' I shouted, and she saw it and stopped.

It was then that I realised that the car now zooming up the drive was one that I knew.

'Heather! Look!' I grabbed her arm, and pointed to the yellow Mini. 'It's Miss Carter!'

If Miss Carter had recognised us, she didn't give any indication. She had a fierce look of grim determination on her granite features.

'Heather! I knew it. I knew there was something weird about this place. You know what this means, don't you?'

'Stop it!'

'What?' I asked, bewildered.

'Stop it. Don't even start it. Don't say anything. Just don't!'

'I was only going to say – '

'Don't. Don't you dare say it!'

'Say what?'

'Don't you dare say anything about aliens!'

'But – '

'No!' She stabbed a finger at me. I'd never seen her so angry. 'If you say one word about aliens I will never ever speak to you again!'

'But Heather – '

'Shut up. Just shut up!'

And with that, she stormed away.

* * * * * * * *

'Who are you trying to ring, Janie?'

I put the receiver down.

'Just Heather. She's not in.'

Mum frowned as she put the plates full of steaming spaghetti on the table.

'Why is it so urgent? You were with her all afternoon!'

I sat down and stared miserably at my food.

'Don't say you two have fallen out?'

Fallen out? We had come back on the same bus, and Heather wouldn't sit with me or speak to me.

'You'll make it up again, Janie. Don't let it ruin your appetite.'

I pushed my fork half-heartedly into my spaghetti.

'So it wasn't a very good trip, then?' said Mum.

I shook my head.

'I suppose you argued about something silly?'

I wondered if I should tell Mum where we had been. I wanted to talk about it – and after all, *I* hadn't been told not to visit Nanna Miller.

'We went to see her nanna.'

'Oh?'

'She lives in a horrible Home. It's like a prison. And she didn't even know who Heather was.'

Mum put her fork down.

'It was awful,' I said.

'I expect it was. Janie – '

'I don't really want to talk about it any more, Mum.'

Mum said nothing more, but kept looking at me in a worried kind of way.

I forced some of the spaghetti down, and then tried to phone Heather again.

Diane answered. Only this time she didn't say, 'She's out!' like she had before.

'Oh, you again, alien. Why don't you get lost? She doesn't want to speak to you. Can't you get the message?'

'Can you tell her – '

'No I can't! She hates you. Go away.'

I sank down onto the bottom stair, my head in my hands. 'Oh God! God – now I've lost my only friend in all the world!'

I didn't try telephoning her again on Sunday. I hoped that she might ring me. She didn't. The phone only rang once, and it was Dad – I don't think he could understand why I sounded so disappointed when I heard his voice.

Worse was to come. Mrs. Bell announced to the class on Monday that Heather Miller was ill and that she probably wouldn't be back to school this term.

The Church On The Hill

Why did the bus always take five minutes to get to school in the morning, and about five hours to get home in the afternoon?

'Someone's mucking around with the time-space vacuum,' I muttered, as I got off at my stop, and I wondered what the time-space vacuum actually was.

Nearly home! I thought as I trudged past the Co-op. A couple of teenagers came out of the shop and I bumped into one of them.

'Sorry,' I mumbled, and kept walking.

'Oh! Look who it is. The alien!'

I hadn't realised that I'd knocked into Diane. She was glaring at me.

'This is an alien,' she said to her friend, a lanky, spotty-faced boy. 'Looks like an alien, doesn't it?'

I was too tired to retaliate.

'How's Heather?'

'She's ill.' Diane opened a can of Coke.

'Tell her I hope she gets well soon.'

'If she gets well it won't be any thanks to you.'

'What?'

Diane drank from the can, and then handed it to the boy. 'You're no friend of hers, alien. If you really were her friend, you would have stopped her from going to see Nanna on Saturday.'

I couldn't think of anything to say.

'That's right, stand there looking stupid, it's what you're best at,' sneered Diane. 'Didn't you know she's not allowed to go and see Nanna? Now it's upset her so much she's had to have the doctor, and *I've* had to stay home and look after her.'

She didn't seem to be dressed for the part of caring nurse, in her tight jeans and very low cut top, but I didn't say so.

'C'mon, Di,' said the boy.

Diane leaned towards me in a threatening manner. 'We'd never have known what was the matter with her if some woman hadn't phoned us from the Home, worried about two girls who visited Nanna and went away upset.'

I took a step backwards.

'You're a bad influence, Jane Collins.'

A wave of sudden indignation swept over me.

'Hold on a minute!' I said. '*I* didn't know there was

anything wrong with your nanna. It's not *my* fault! Heather just didn't think it was fair she couldn't see her nanna, just because your mum's got a problem!'

'You what!'

'Your mum. She didn't want Heather to see your nanna because she's your dad's – '

'You liar!' Diane shrieked. 'That's not true! My mum hasn't got a problem! Nanna is *senile*, and Mum didn't want Heather to know!'

'C'mon, Di,' said the boy.

'Heather doesn't like you any more. You and your silly stories! You're just a – a – ' she tossed her hair, and stared down her nose at me. 'Just a child. That's all. A child.'

'C'mon,' said the boy.

'Child!'

Diane and the boy drifted off down an alleyway. I still felt indignant. Fancy saying I was a bad influence! What a cheek!

Still, I felt sorry for Heather. I'd been thinking about her all day. We'd all signed a get well card for her that afternoon, and Mrs. Bell was going to deliver it. I'd signed the card, 'Your best friend, Jane' and was annoyed to see that Olivia Gates had already signed, 'Your best friend, Olivia'.

As I walked home, I told myself that I'd been quite brave, really, answering Diane back. She was much bigger than me, and she'd been very aggressive. Perhaps I really would turn out like Sandra Richmond when I grew up. I began to have a pleasant fantasy where I was being congratulated by the head teacher, applauded for the success of my wonderful career. I could see myself standing on the stage in the great hall, hundreds of girls clapping me.

'Jane has just come back to say goodbye to us before going off to work on the new Mars Space Station. She's only twenty-four, but she's been promoted to the rank of Colonel – '

But I swiftly dismissed the fantasy as the thought of my very poor performance in science came to mind. I would certainly have to do something about my complete lack of ability to grasp the fundamentals of chemistry and physics before I became an astronaut. We had had a physics exam that day, and I hadn't even understood the questions. Heather was missing the exams. I envied her. I supposed Olivia would be top again in everything. I was thinking about Olivia and her malicious remarks towards me when I walked into the kitchen.

'Thank you very much!' I heard Mum say, from the hall.

'All right, love.'

A man's voice! Who was that? Not my dad!

'Goodbye!'

I peeped over Mum's shoulder. A burly man with a large canvas bag was lumbering down the drive.

'Who was that, Mum?'

'Mr. Ives from up the road. He's a plumber. He's fixed the toilet.'

'I thought Dad was going to do that?'

Mum shut the front door.

'Janie, I'm afraid your dad won't be coming home again for quite a while.'

* * * * * * * *

'Something's happened to this hill,' I said to myself, as I got off my bike and started to push it. 'It never used to be so steep!'

It was very hot, even in the early evening, and my hair was damp with sweat. There it was, huge and awesome, a great spire with a cross on the top reaching to the sky. I took a deep breath, screwing up my courage. I was going into that church. Yes, I was. It had taken me several days to pluck up my nerve to go to the church, but I had come to the conclusion that I just had to do it.

I didn't think God could have heard my last prayer for help. I wondered where I was going wrong with my prayers. After all, the first time I'd prayed, he had answered. I tried to recall how I'd prayed that first time. Maybe there was a set formula to this praying thing; perhaps there were certain words God liked you to use.

If I *was* using the right words, it was very likely that God had been very busy and just hadn't got round to me yet. It struck me that prayers might be like planes at an airport, circling and circling, coming down one by one. Mine apparently hadn't come down yet.

I was going to pray again. The more prayers I had circling around, the better it would be. And if there were certain words I ought to use, I would probably get more of an idea what they were if I was in a church. They might be written down somewhere. At any rate, going to church would show God that I was deadly serious about wanting my prayers answered.

I wheeled my bike through the little roofed gate of the churchyard. Gazing into the blue heavens, I wondered if my prayer was flying about up there. Well, I was going to give it a helping hand. I couldn't wait for thousands of other prayers to flop onto God's doormat first.

There were lots of headstones, some falling forward,

some half covered in weeds. Fleetingly, I tried to imagine Sandra Richmond going to church. No – she wouldn't go. She wouldn't have the time.

I propped my bike against the church wall. I went into the porch, and looked up at the heavy oak door. This was it. The big moment. What if the door wouldn't open? Well, I decided, I would just have to pray to God in the porch. Just as I was about to reach for the massive handle, the door opened, and a willowy woman in a pink dress came out, carrying an armful of dead flowers. I don't know which one of us was the more surprised.

'Oh! Can I help you?'

'Can I go in?'

'Do you want to see someone?'

'Mmm... kind of.'

'Was it the vicar you wanted?'

'No.'

'Well, who then?'

'God.'

She nearly dropped the flowers.

'God?'

'God,' I said, firmly.

'You'd better go in, then.'

I slipped past her, and stopped in the doorway as I

took in the splendour of the building. There was a musty, old sort of smell. The high ceiling looked like the hull of an ancient sailing ship turned upside down. I tried to forget the size of any spiders that might be hanging around up there ready to drop down my neck.

'Have you been here before?' the willowy woman asked.

'I've been to church before – my school has a carol service every Christmas at St. Catherine's in the town.'

'But you've never been to this church before?'

A wave of apprehension swept over me.

'Is it all right?' I said. 'I mean, is it all right for me to be here?'

She smiled warmly. 'It's fine,' she said, and patted my arm. Then she took her flowers outside, and left me alone in the church. The central aisle had pews either side, and at the end of the aisle was a rail; beyond that, a table covered in a white cloth with gold edging held three silver crosses. On the left, right down the front, was the pulpit. Glancing around, I saw bunches of fresh flowers everywhere. I recognised the font at the back.

But it wasn't the font that I wanted, or the pulpit, or the table with crosses on it. I wanted God. I walked purposefully up the aisle, my footsteps making a dull thud on the tiled floor. I strode past the pews, and up two steps, and then walked past seats which faced each other.

The front piece by the rail was carpeted. I guessed this was where you had to pray. Did I have to kneel? I looked behind me. No one about. I dropped down onto my knees. Now, what words to say? I wanted to say the right thing. Perhaps I should have asked the willowy woman. I let my eyes wander – I might see a stack of pre-written prayers, or at least instructions on how to pray, lying around somewhere. But no. Then I looked up.

There was a beautiful stained glass window above the table with the crosses on it. It was so lovely, I couldn't understand how I hadn't noticed it as soon as I'd walked into the church. Evening sunlight was setting ablaze ruby reds, sapphire blues, and bright yellows. The colours were so intense, they didn't seem to quite belong to this earth. And there, in the middle of all the beauty, was a figure.

It was Jesus. He was wearing a long white robe, and he was carrying a lamb in his arms. He looked very serious, and his hair was blond instead of brown like it was in my little Jesus book. A halo shone over his head, and above that, the words: 'The Good Shepherd'. Beneath his feet was a scroll, and on it was written,

'Come unto Me'. I stared at the stained glass window for a long time. Eventually, I realised my knees were sore, and I stood up, my eyes still fixed on the window.

'Gorgeous, isn't it?'

I jumped. The willowy woman was just behind me.

'I've got to go,' I said.

'Come again.'

I walked back down the aisle, and suddenly remembered that I had come here to pray. I hadn't prayed at all. I hadn't said one word to God... yet I knew, somehow, we had communicated there in that church. Outside, I leaned on the handlebars of my bike, and gazed across the streets and buildings below. What marvellous peace I felt! It was like a warm blanket, covering me from the top of my head to the soles of my feet.

I'll go and see Heather tomorrow, I decided. Surely she will have got over being cross with me by then.

A yellow car sped past the church, and I thought of Miss Carter turning up at the old people's Home. What *had* she been doing there?

Things Get Worse

Splosh, splosh. Splashing through the puddles, I began to whistle. It had been raining all day – thunder, lightning, gloomy grey skies – but I didn't care. I was going to visit Heather.

It was only when I arrived at Heather's house that my own personal sunshine hid behind a cloud. There, by the gate, was another bike.

'Olivia Gates!'

And there she was, thin pony-tail bouncing down the drive.

'Oh!' she said, when she saw me.

I said nothing. I wheeled my bike past her.

'Well, they won't let you see her!' she called.

'Why not?' I turned to her, defensively.

'She's not well enough.'

'*I'm* her best friend.'

'Just telling you.' She got onto her bike. 'Anyway, you're not. Diane says Heather doesn't like you any more. I don't think she ever liked you. She just felt sorry for you.'

I gripped the handlebars, and opened my mouth to say something nasty to her, but she was talking again.

'Diane says it's half your fault Heather's so sick, anyway.'

'What!'

'You encouraged her to do wrong,' said Olivia, pompously.

'I encouraged her to –'

'And Diane says there's something wrong with you. She says Heather told her you thought Miss Carter was an alien from outer space.'

I could feel myself blush.

'Don't you know that Miss Carter's mother is in Hollytrees Home? She nearly died last week, Mrs. Bell told us. Didn't you hear her? No – of course not. You were either daydreaming as usual, or having one of your days off.' And with one last smug smile, she pedalled off.

As she disappeared from view, Heather's front door opened. Steve was coming out, with the lanky boy I'd seen with Diane.

'Oh, shut up!' Steve was yelling into the house, and the door slammed behind him.

'You know your trouble, don't you?' the lanky boy

said, as they sauntered up to me. 'You live in a house full of women. You want to get out of there.'

'You're telling me!'

They strolled past as if I wasn't there.

'She can't stop me going on holiday, though,' Steve said, 'and I'm going, all right, whether she likes it or not.'

I watched his yellow head bobbing along behind the hedge as he and his friend ambled off in the opposite direction to Olivia.

'He didn't even notice me!' I said, and I felt completely crushed.

'Oi! Oi!'

Someone was shouting out of an upstairs window. I recognised the voice, and I could see Diane leaning out.

'Get off our property! Go on, get off!'

'I was only – '

'Go away! She won't see you. You make her worse!'

I jumped on my bike and raced for home. Olivia's comments whirled in my brain – 'It's half your fault Heather's so sick!' was the phrase that hurt me most. And then there was Diane – 'You make her worse!' On top of that, Steve hadn't noticed me. He didn't even know I was alive.

Your fault! Your fault! Terrible words... was it my fault, after all, that Heather was so ill? Was it, really? Was I a bad influence? Yes, I did tell her stories about aliens, and I'd known we should have got permission to see her nanna... but surely, I hadn't caused her illness? No, it was silly to think that. Wasn't it?

A car's horn sounded.

'Stupid kid!'

He was right. I *was* stupid. Everybody thought so. There was something wrong with me. And Heather had only been my friend because she'd felt sorry for me.

It was raining hard by the time I got home, and Mum exclaimed, 'Oh Janie!' as I dripped into the kitchen.

'I'll go and change.'

'I *did* tell you to take – '

But I didn't want to talk, or get lectured, or be told a thousand reasons why I shouldn't have got so wet. I retreated to the safety of my bedroom, and threw myself down on the bed.

I shot straight up again as I realised that I'd made my bed wet.

'Janie!'

'I'm changing!'

'Let me have those wet things!'

I opened my door a fraction, shoved my wet clothes out, and shut the door again.

'Janie!'

'I'm doing my revision!'

That was a lie. I was actually feeling my damp duvet and hoping Mum wouldn't come in.

I sighed with relief as I heard her go down the stairs. I threw myself onto the bed again, and buried my face in the pillow.

'Oh God!'

I could hear the rain against my window.

'Oh God!'

It dawned on me why God hadn't answered my prayers. Why would he want to? I was just a stupid kid – worse than that, a bad stupid kid. I turned over, and stared at the ceiling. Yes, that was it. I was bad. Really bad. What was it Olivia had said? I'd encouraged Heather to do wrong, and now my friend was ill, and things were worse than ever. Dad wasn't coming again for a long time – if he ever came home at all. Maybe that was it, he had gone for good, never coming back.

Then there were the exams. I'd made a complete mess of them so far. All the days off I'd had for sicknesses real or imaginary had left great gaping holes in my education. I couldn't revise what I hadn't learned. We only had a couple of exams left, and one of those was geography.

Life just couldn't get any worse. Could it?

It was very dark. It was very cold.

Sandra felt the gun in her back, as she was pushed into the cell.

'You'll pay for this, Careless Carter,' said Sandra. The alien laughed — a high-pitched cackling laugh. It made Sandra shiver.

'Now you're my prisoner. You'll never get away!'

'Don't be too sure of that,' replied Sandra. 'You know who you're dealing with!'

'Look around you, Colonel Richmond. How do you think you'll ever escape from this place? It's just not possible.'

Heavy manacles were on Sandra's wrists now. She was shackled to the wall.

'You won't get away with this, Careless!'

More laughter.

'Oh, I think we have got away with it, Colonel Richmond! We're in control. We've got Mr. Collins, we've got Heather Miller. And there's nothing you can do about it!'

Sandra Richmond gritted her teeth, and pulled at the iron chains. It was no use. She was trapped.

'Paul Sinclaire will come to my rescue! Oh — no he won't. I forgot. He's on holiday.'

'Goodbye, Colonel. We won't meet again. I will be avenged for my darling Zoggo! We'll conquer the earth. And it'll be your fault. All your fault!'

'My fault!'

'Yes, you're a bad influence, Sandra Richmond. You make people sick. And now I must go, I've got to visit my mother.'

The cell door heaved and groaned and then shut tight, and Sandra could hear bolts being bolted, locks being locked. The last glimmer of light disappeared as Careless Carter drew a shutter down over the peep-hole in the door.

'Oh,' said Sandra, 'what a nuisance!'

Something ran across the cold stone floor.

'Rats!'

She couldn't see them, but she could hear them.

'Nuisance!' said Sandra. She pulled at the chains again.

'If only I had a nail file on me!' But she had no nail fail, and no means of escape. Then, she realised that she wasn't alone in the cell. She heard a clink-clink of another pair of iron shackles.

'Well, I know the aliens haven't shackled the rats to the wall, because the little beasts are running about,' muttered Sandra, 'so it must be someone else.'

There was a faint moan, now, from the other side of the cell.

'Hello! Who's there? Speak up.' Another moan. 'Don't despair, we'll be free of this in no time. You don't have a nail file by any chance, do you?'

Suddenly, there was a shaft of eerie light in the cell. It was moonlight, coming from a vertical slit high in the wall. Sandra narrowed her eyes. She could just make out a little bundle wrapped up in a purple cardigan.

'Nanna? Nanna Miller?'

The old head moved, and Sandra could see the face clearly. But it wasn't Nanna Miller.

'Gran! Gran! Gran!'

'Janie!'

There was a blinding light, and I sat up.

'Mum! Mum! Is that you?'

'Yes, Janie. Calm down!"

My heart was thumping.

'Oh, Mum, I've had a terrible dream.'

'I heard you shouting.' Mum yawned. 'It's one o'clock in the morning, Janie. I thought we had burglars.'

'Burglars!'

'Oh, don't start worrying about burglars, now! Just go back to sleep.' Mum snapped off the light.

I switched on my bedside lamp. My heart was still pounding. I heard Mum get back into her creaky old bed. The rain had stopped. The moon was shining into my room, hanging in the dark sky like a great white ball.

That dream! That horrible dream! I tried to dismiss it from my mind, but it wouldn't go.

That little bundle wrapped in a purple cardigan in Sandra's cell. That ancient face. Those faded eyes.

'Gran.'

My gran was in that prison cell with Sandra Richmond. *My* gran – not Heather's nanna. My wonderful, kind gran, so full of life – reduced to a bundle of rags; scared, trapped, unrecognisable.

But it was only a dream.

Wasn't it?

I had a dreadful thought. What if my gran was in a Home, just like Nanna Miller? Perhaps that was why we didn't go to see her. Maybe my gran had got so old, so frail, so ill that she didn't know who anyone was any more; was that why Mum had been praying, and why Dad didn't come home? Was it something to do with Gran?

'Don't be daft,' I said, out loud, 'Dad said he'd seen Gran and that she was all right, and had lots of her friends round at her place. Come on, Jane. You're just being silly.'

Clouds obscured the moon. It was going to rain again.

'I suppose Dad wasn't just *saying* that?'

Thunder rumbled in the distance. I got out of bed, and quickly drew the curtains. Something malevolent was out there. It was lurking. It was ready to pounce.

Aliens, I thought; the unseen enemy! They're stepping up the fight! 'Oh God!' I looked at the little Jesus book that was lying on my bedside table. I grabbed it, and held it to my chest. Maybe God didn't hear me – maybe he didn't want to. But I had no one else to turn to. No one else could help. Sandra Richmond couldn't help me, could she? No, she wasn't real, she was only in my imagination, and even in *that* she was in prison with no means of escape.

But God was real. I knew it. He was my only hope. 'Oh God. Oh God. Oh – Jesus!'

I sat for a long time on the edge of my bed, staring at, but not seeing, the little book. Then, I realised that I had opened it, although I couldn't remember doing it.

In front of me was a picture of Jesus, carrying a lamb, just like he had been in the stained glass window. Only this time, the words accompanying the picture were: *'Do not be afraid, little flock, for your Father has been pleased to give you the kingdom.'*

And did I imagine it? I felt a real sense of peace settle in my room, just like the kind of peace I had felt when I'd been to the church. And I knew one thing was for sure. The situation wasn't hopeless. God knew about it. He knew about me. And he cared.

A Brilliant Idea

'Jane! Jane Collins!'

I heard the swift click-click of high heels coming down the corridor. I looked over my shoulder, very reluctantly.

'Yes, Mrs. Bell?'

'Jane. I want to speak to you.'

So did most of the teachers in the school. My exam results had been appalling.

Mrs. Bell gripped my arm and led me into the nearest classroom. Unhappily, it happened to be the geography room.

She shut the door, and I gazed at the maps. It should have been the happiest day of the year for me. It was the last day of term.

The summer holidays stretched out ahead.

'Jane, you're not very happy, are you?'

I eyed the floor.

'Come on, Jane. You can talk to me.'

I raised my eyes, and saw that she looked genuinely concerned.

'I'm all right, thank you, Mrs. Bell,' I said, half-heartedly.

'Jane. Your exam results.'

'Yes, Mrs. Bell?'

'You haven't done very well, have you?'

That was an understatement.

'No, Mrs. Bell.'

'I'm afraid your report isn't all it should be.'

It was in my bag. I had been wondering if I could lose it on the way home.

Mrs. Bell folded her arms. 'Jane, St. Catherine's is a good school. Most of our girls go on to further education. Many of them go to the best universities.'

Further education! I exclaimed, inwardly. I find ordinary education hard enough!

'Jane, do you know *why* you don't like St. Catherine's?'

My gaze locked with hers. My secret was out. The teachers knew.

'We don't want you to be unhappy. If there's a problem, you should tell us. You can always talk to me – you should know that.'

'Yes, Mrs. Bell.'

'I know that some girls don't do so well here. They find the standard of work a bit high.'

Now she was calling me an idiot.

'Don't look like that, Jane. I know you're not stupid! I'm just trying to explain that the disciplined academic atmosphere that we have at St. Catherine's doesn't suit everyone. Some people tend to flourish in less strict surroundings. Do you see?'

'Yes.' Fear gripped me. What was she saying? That I should leave? My parents would be devastated. They had been so proud when I'd won a place at St. Catherine's – such a famous old school!

'Oh, don't worry. I'm not suggesting you go to another school! You see, I don't believe that the work here is too hard for you. Do you know what I think?'

I shook my head.

'I think you just don't try.'

'Oh.'

'Your work is careless, Jane. But I think, if you tried, you'd be pretty good. In fact, I think you'd be above the class average in most subjects – except perhaps in science. I know you could be near the top – or top – in English.'

'Oh!'

'I would really like to see what you could do if you put your mind to it. But will you do that, Jane? Really try?'

I looked at my watch. 'I'm going to miss my bus.'

Mrs. Bell sighed. 'Oh, well. I just want you to remember – we want to help you. We aren't your enemies, you know!'

'Mmm.'

'I'm going your way, Jane. I'll give you a lift home. I'm going to visit Heather.'

Mrs. Bell studied my face.

'Jane, is there another problem? I mean – apart from school?'

'No.'

'All right, Jane. Come on.'

I followed her out to the car park. It was very embarrassing to be given a lift home by a teacher – but I *had* missed my bus. I was relieved that most people had gone home, so there was nobody who knew me to stand and stare as I went home with Mrs. Bell.

Miss Carter's yellow Mini was parked next to Mrs. Bell's car. The geography teacher was unlocking the Mini's boot, and shoving papers and books inside.

'End of term at last!' commented Mrs. Bell.

Miss Carter looked up, and saw me.

'Have a lovely holiday, Jane!'

She smiled at me. I was shocked. She waved as she climbed into the Mini, and drove off. I was still in shock when I got in beside Mrs. Bell. Miss Carter had smiled. She had smiled at me. I had never seen her smile before. Could it be that Miss Carter was human after all?

'Jane?'

'Yes?'

'Did you hear what I said?'

'Oh, sorry, no, I didn't, Mrs. Bell.'

Mrs. Bell glanced at me as we pulled out into traffic. 'I said, have you any idea what you would like to do when you leave school?'

Celebrate, I thought.

'Most people have one or two ideas, even if they change them later on. What about you, Jane?'

I decided to tell her what I had told no one else.

'I want to join the Space Programme at NASA. Be an astronaut.'

Mrs. Bell fell in a laughing heap over her steering wheel, and we nearly went through a red light.

'Oh, Jane! You do have a sense of humour!'

'I'm being serious.'

She looked at me, and tried to compose herself.

'The light's green,' I pointed out. We were off again.

'Is it true what Heather said?' Mrs. Bell asked. 'You've written a book?'

'Well – I'm still writing it.'

'And it's about – '

'It's a science fiction story.'

'Science fiction! That explains NASA!' Mrs. Bell nodded. 'What's the plot?'

I told her.

'I'll tell you what, Jane,' she said, as we arrived in Willow Drive, 'why don't you forget all about joining NASA, and being an astronaut, and think about being a journalist, or a writer?'

It was a new idea.

'Mrs. Bell,' I said, suddenly, 'you know you said if I tried, I could be above the class average in most things – except for science – what about geography?'

'Miss Carter thinks you have a perfectly good brain, and could quite easily cope with the work. That's why she gets so annoyed with you – you could do so much better.'

I slammed the car door shut. Mrs. Bell leant across the passenger seat, and opened the window.

'If you attended school more regularly, you'd find school life a lot easier. Oh, and Jane – next term, I would love to read your book.'

Mum was in the back garden, digging a hole in one of the borders. My heart sank. I had to give her the report.

'That's it,' I said, 'Freedom.'

Mum straightened her back, and leaned on the spade. 'You don't look too happy about it!' she said.

'What are you doing?'

'Planting.'

'Shall I put the kettle on?'

'Janie – '

'Oh, all right. Here it is.' I rummaged in my school bag, and handed her my report.

I watched her face fall as she read it.

'Oh dear,' she said.

'I'll put the kettle on.'

'No. Janie – this report – '

'I know.'

'Oh dear.'

'Are you going to show it to Dad?'

'Of course!'

'Always supposing he ever comes home again.' I turned to go indoors.

'Janie! That's not fair. You know your dad's been very busy lately. He's hoping to come home soon.'

'I bet.'

'Jane!'

'I'm tired.'

Mum was right behind me as I walked into the kitchen.

'Janie, I'm very worried about you. You've been very quiet recently.'

'I've had exams.'

'But they're over.'

'I'm OK, Mum.'

'No, you're not. Your report says as much.'

'Oh, Mum!' I said, exasperated. 'I *hate* that school!'

'It's a good school!'

'I *hate* it.' I slumped down at the kitchen table.

'Janie, some people would give their eyeteeth to go to St. Catherine's.'

'Yes, there are a lot of weird people about.'

Mum sat down opposite me.

'Do you really hate it?'

'Yes, I do.'

'I thought you found the work hard. Can't you cope?'

'I hate it.' I put my head down on my arms.

'I expect you're worried about Heather.'

'No, why should I be? I only made her ill, and she won't speak to me any more.'

'What?' Mum touched my arm. 'Made her ill? What do you mean?'

'You know I told you we went to see her nanna? Well, we shouldn't have gone. Heather wasn't allowed. I should have stopped her, because it made her ill. I'm a bad influence. I am, Mum. I'm a bad influence.'

'You're just tired.'

'Yes, and a bad influence.'

'That's not true.'

'It *is* true.'

'Janie, I know you shouldn't have gone to see Heather's nanna. I've known it for some time.'

'What? How – '

'I've spoken to Mrs. Miller.'

I gazed at her, and she smiled.

'I was going to talk to you about it once the exams were over, but you've been a bit off-colour, haven't you? I thought I'd leave it for a while.'

'When did you speak to Mrs. Miller?'

'Just after you told me where you and Heather had been. I bumped into her in the Co-op, and we had quite a chat.'

I tried to say something, but the words wouldn't come.

'It's true you shouldn't have gone to the Home, but the shock of seeing her nanna so poorly was just the final straw for Heather. There's been a lot of strain at home, because of the divorce.' Mum squeezed my arm. 'You're not to blame for Heather's illness, Janie. Mrs. Miller is blaming herself.'

'It was horrible at that Home, Mum. It was like a prison.'

'Janie, the Home is made secure like that for the good of the residents! It's for their own safety. Some of them don't really know what they're doing, and they can just wander off and hurt themselves. Nobody wants that to happen.'

'Nanna Miller didn't know what she was doing, Mum. She didn't even recognise Heather.'

Mum nodded. 'Yes, so I heard. Mrs. Miller said that she didn't tell Heather her nanna was so unwell because she thought Heather wouldn't really understand. It's all backfired a bit. Poor Mrs. Miller. She's feeling so awful about it all.'

'But Mum,' I said, as a lump appeared in my throat, 'Heather won't speak to me.'

'I don't think she wants to speak to anyone – not just yet. Give her some time, Janie, and she'll be fine.'

Mum sat back in her seat, and eyed me thoughtfully. 'Perhaps the school will understand that it was worry about Heather – '

'Oh, Mum, it's not just that!' Hot tears trickled down my cheeks.

'Come on, Janie. What is it?'

I wanted to talk about Dad. I wanted to say, 'Are you going to split up?' – but I couldn't.

'I do hate St. Catherine's!' I choked.

Mum was still holding my report, and she glanced down at it.

'We were so proud when you won a place at St. Catherine's!' she said, sadly. 'But you've never done well there, have you? Not as well as – '

'Not as well as you'd hoped.'

'You know, Janie, your gran always wanted me to go to a really good school, but I was never clever enough.'

I thought about Gran, and suddenly I longed to see her. 'Mum, can we go and see Gran? Please?'

'That's not possible at the moment, Janie. It's too far to go for a day trip. We'd have to go on the train.'

'Can't we? Can't we do that?' I wanted to go to Gran's more than anything in the world. I wanted to see her. And I wanted to get away from Gipley.

Mum smiled, and lifted her eyes. As she looked at me, her expression changed. It became very serious.

'Why shouldn't we go? There's no real reason, is there? We *will* go. We'll catch the train, and perhaps stay one or two days, if that's all right with Gran.' She clapped her hands. 'Yes, why not? Brilliant idea, Janie!'

She went off to phone Gran, and came back with a broad grin. We were going to Gran's for a week!

'I'll let your dad know. He might be able to come and see us – Gran's is so much nearer his office than Gipley is.'

Thank you, God, I thought. Thank you, thank you, thank you.

'Sandra! Sandra Richmond!'

Sandra opened her eyes. She'd had no food, no water, nothing, for a long, long time.

'Hello?' she said. 'Who's calling me?'

There was a bright light in the cell. It wasn't moonlight. It was coming from what appeared to be an open door. Only the door wasn't the door she'd come in by — the one that the alien had shut tight.

Sandra realised that her wrists weren't bound by the chains any more. She could stand up. She did, and was surprised to find new strength flowing through her body.

'This is very odd!' said Sandra, glancing back at her cell. It was empty. Her companion in the purple cardigan had disappeared.

'Very odd indeed!'

She looked at the open door. What was beyond it? She didn't know.

Colonel Sandra Richmond, Space Force's greatest pilot, straightened her uniform.

'Is this a rescue attempt?'

No one answered.

'Is this a rescue attempt? Hello? If it is a rescue attempt, I have to tell you, I've never been rescued before. I'm usually the one doing the rescuing!'

Still no answer.

Oh well, she thought, stepping forward.

Into the unknown!

Strangers

'You look great. Really well. Do you feel well? You look well.'

Gran stopped what she was doing, and stared at me, exasperated. 'Jane! Will you stop asking me if I feel all right? You're giving me a complex.'

'But you look so well, Gran.'

'That's wonderful, and I'm glad you think so, and I feel absolutely marvellous. But if you ask me one more time if I feel well, I will do something drastic!'

I giggled. Her laughing eyes twinkled at me, and she carried on feeding the birds.

'I do love it here!' I exclaimed, smiling as I gazed around the familiar square patch of lawn that was Gran's garden.

'And I love having you here!' said Gran.

Already birds were gathering in neighbouring trees, anticipating the feast to come. Gran ushered me back indoors, and we watched the birds come down for their breakfast. This was a ritual I remembered from years ago, when I was tiny. Feed the birds, then watch them. The familiarity of it was very comforting.

'It's going to be hot today,' said Gran. 'Make sure the birds have plenty of water while I'm out, won't you, Jane? I keep topping up the bird bath but the little rascals will sit in it.'

'How long will you be, Gran?'

'Hour and a half or so. Not long.'

There were just a few clouds in the sky. Cumulus, I thought. Was it Cumulus – fluffy clouds? I had to admit, *some* geography could be *fairly* interesting.

'Jane? Did you hear me?'

'Sorry, Gran?'

'You're miles away! I was just saying, I've invited some people for lunch.'

'What a glorious morning!' Mum appeared in the doorway, clutching a carton of milk, some eggs and a newspaper. 'I'd almost forgotten how peaceful Tamsford is. Mind you, there have been a few changes since we were last here. Those new houses down by the village green, and the huge conservatory at the Manse. Oh, and someone has painted the pub a most peculiar shade of pink.'

'Times change,' said Gran. 'They call it progress.'

'Progress? I'd call the pink pub a bit of a nightmare.'

'I was telling Jane about the guests I've invited for lunch.'

'Oh, yes, Jane,' said Mum, a little breezily, 'Gran has asked some of her friends over, and I'm going to prepare the meal.'

'You don't have to do that, Julie,' said Gran. 'The offer still stands – you could come to church with me, and we'll have a late lunch.'

'Oh, no, that's all right. I don't mind. Really, It will be like saying a big thank you for having us at such short notice.'

'Well, would Jane like to come?'

'Oh no, she wouldn't be interested. Would you, Janie?'

'I – '

'We've got a good Bible Class, Jane,' Gran told me.

Unfortunately, that was the worse thing she could have said. Bible Class sounded too much like school for my liking.

'There was no need to look so horrified at the thought of going to church!' Mum said to me, later, as we waved Gran goodbye. 'Honestly, Janie. You know church is important to your gran.'

'I *wasn't* horrified!'

'You should have seen your face. Now, I'm going to start preparing lunch... although where we're going to eat it, I don't know.'

We both looked round at the minuscule living room-cum-dining room. Gran's old cottage was so tiny, it seemed crowded with just the three of us. It was crammed full of tables, shelves, stools, knick-knacks, chairs that didn't match, and piles and piles of books and magazines stacked on the carpets in every room – even the bathroom. It was as if the contents of a much bigger house had been shovelled into this little one – which actually was the case, because Gran had moved here just after Grandad died.

'Who has Gran invited to lunch?' I asked.

'Some of her friends from church.'

'Yes, but who?'

'A couple of elderly widows and a young woman. Gran arranged it all before she knew we were coming.'

'Do you think they'll be weird?'

'Why on earth should they be?'

I sniggered. 'You know what Dad says about Gran's friends.'

'Why don't you go upstairs and finish unpacking? You must have lots to do.'

'You think they're going to be weird, don't you!'

'Go upstairs. I'll give you weird.'

I bounded up the narrow staircase, into the sloping-roofed box room that Gran called bedroom number three. I sat down on the lemon-coloured duvet and giggled. I thought about Dad's facetious remarks about Gran's friends. But I stopped laughing when I remembered they were church people. I supposed they would carry Bibles and be very serious. Worse – they might ask me difficult questions, or try to persuade Mum to make me go to a Bible Class.

I hadn't had time to unpack all my things when we arrived yesterday. I put some of my T-shirts in an ancient chest of drawers, and I hung a shirt in the dark cupboard that was pretending to be a wardrobe. Then I brought out my story, and placed it on top of the chest of drawers. I hadn't had room for my radio, so I wouldn't be able to discover if the alien bleep! bleep! noises extended as far as Essex.

However, I had found room for my Jesus book. I put it on the windowsill, and looked out across Gran's handkerchief garden, right into the bedroom of the cottage opposite. It wasn't the same as staring into the vast, lonely open space behind our house in Gipley – besides, not everyone likes having thirteen year olds staring into their bedrooms. My day-dreaming out of the open window would have to stop for a week. Oh well! I carried on unpacking.

I knew lunch was ready when a delicious smell wafted upstairs. It coincided with a lot of noise and a slamming front door. Mum had timed lunch to perfection – Gran's guests had arrived.

'Janie! Janie! Come and meet Gran's friends!'

I heard something panting, and I frowned. Gran's friends sounded weirder than I'd expected.

'Janie – come and meet Zero.'

Zero! My heart skipped a beat. That was an odd name for an elderly widow.

I don't suppose... I don't suppose there's something unearthly going on? I wondered. Surely not! Gran seemed her usual self. There couldn't be an alien presence in Tamsford. Could there?

Gingerly, I crept down the stairs – only to be greeted at the bottom by a great, hairy black animal that jumped up to welcome me, putting two massive paws on my chest.

'Ah, you've met Zero!' said Gran.

'Whose dog is he?' I asked.

'Sarah's. Where is Sarah?'

'Out in the garden with the others,' said Mum. The two of them were struggling with Gran's dining table, which was half buried under books, magazines, and a hideous blue vase.

The black dog ran off into the garden.

'Go and say hello to them!' said Gran. 'They're dying to meet you, Jane! Go and introduce yourself!'

'Must I?'

'Janie, don't be so rude!' said Mum.

I went into the kitchen, and peered out at the guests. I had never met any of Gran's church friends before. Somehow, we had always managed to avoid them when we visited. And now, there they were, standing in Gran's garden, looking perfectly happy – and not carrying Bibles. There were two old women, one chatting away, apparently not stopping to take a breath. The younger woman was nodding politely, and smiling, and patting Zero's head.

They were coming in.

'Hello!' I said, brightly. Three pairs of eyes were fixed on me.

'Hello!' said Gran's friends, in unison.

'I'm Jane.'

'Thought so!' said the younger woman, with a grin.

The other two just stared at me. I stared back. I recognised them.

Oh, I had never met them before. But I knew them from Dad's very accurate description of Gran's strange friends. What had he said?

One of them looked dead... yes, that was the skinny one, standing like a statue, white-faced and silent. And the one that had asked Dad if he 'believed' – he had said she was ancient, very intense, and had beedy little eyes. She was the one who had been chatting outside. Those beedy eyes were on me right now.

'Well, Jane! We've heard so much about you.'

'Yes, indeed!' said the white-faced woman, in a whisper.

'We were talking about you before Mrs. Rose here crash-landed.'

'What!'

'Crash-landed, Jane. She slipped up on her way out of church this morning.'

'Oh!'

'I'm Mrs. Day.'

I smiled at her, and she nodded towards the young woman.

'And this is Sarah. Sarah Tanner.'

'Hello!' said Sarah Tanner, with another grin. I liked that grin.

I don't know how we all squeezed round the table. Lots of Gran's bits and pieces had been cast aside and piled up all around us, so there wasn't much room to manoeuvre. Gran said a prayer before we ate, and the old ladies said, 'Amen to that!' and Sarah added, 'Yes, Amen!' and the three of them tucked into the chicken as if they hadn't had a meal for a week. Gran smiled at Mum, and I smiled, too, partly with relief. Any sneaking thoughts about aliens had disappeared when I saw Gran's friends start on the chicken.

I needn't have worried about being asked difficult questions. Mrs. Day did most of the talking throughout the meal, and she didn't pause to ask anyone anything. I was quite happy with that. My only problem was Zero. He had parked himself under the table near me, and every time I looked down, he was staring up with big brown eyes – and dribbling.

It was as Gran dished up the dessert that I began to wonder why a group of church people weren't talking about God. I felt ever so slightly disappointed, because although I didn't want to heard a load of stuff about religion and what I should and shouldn't be doing (especially anything about the dreaded Bible Class) I *was* interested in God, and wanted to know more about him.

I was thinking about this when Mrs. Rose gasped, and fell forward, narrowly missing a splashdown in the trifle.

'Oh, she's always doing this! Fainting!' exclaimed Mrs. Day.

'Oh dear!' Gran rushed out to the kitchen, and returned with a wet cloth.

Sarah Tanner kept on eating. I was very impressed. I thought Sandra Richmond would probably keep on eating when faced with a crisis. In fact, as Gran flopped the cloth into Mrs. Rose's face, it occurred to me that Sarah Tanner was quite like how I imagined Sandra to be, in several ways. Sarah was older than twenty-four – she could even have been as old as thirty, I wasn't sure – but she had the same sort of auburn colouring, and there was a very confident air about her.

'Are you all right, dear?' Gran was asking Mrs. Rose.

'I think I'd like to visit the toilet!' said Mrs. Rose.

'More trifle, Sarah?' Mrs. Day said, briskly.

'Yes, please.'

'Your dog's just been sick under the table,' I said.

'Cancel the trifle,' said Sarah, frowning at Zero, 'I'd better get him outside. He looks a bit odd.'

'Don't worry about the mess,' said Mum, valiantly. 'I'll clear it up.'

'That smell of dog sick is making *me* feel faint, now,' said Mrs. Day, fanning herself with her hand.

'Are you all right, Jane?' Mum asked. 'You're looking very green.'

'I think I'll take him for a walk, stop him messing up the garden.' Sarah turned to me. 'Want to come?'

'Yes,' I said. 'Yes, I would, please.'

I was glad to get out of the cottage. The mixture of dog dribble, dog sick, and old ladies fainting had made me feel quite strange.

I felt better as we walked along. Sarah didn't talk. She didn't put her dog on a lead, either, but then, Gran did live in a very quiet lane. Sarah strode ahead of me, hands deep in her jeans pockets, and she started to whistle a catchy little tune I'd never heard before.

'What a lunch!' she said, at last, and grinned.

I grinned back.

We turned down the leafy path at the end of Gran's lane. Ahead of us were meadows, and the river, and beyond that, combine harvesters were working in golden fields.

'So, you're on holiday?' said Sarah.

'Yes.'

'What's your school like?'

'Horrible.'

'Yeah?'

'I hate it.'

'Yeah, I hated school, too.'

I was beginning to like Sarah.

'Got lots of friends?'

'No.'

'What – no friends at all?'

'I've got one friend. Well, I used to, but she doesn't like me any more. Her name's Heather.'

'Why doesn't she like you any more?'

'Well – ' I hesitated, but soon I was telling her all about Heather's nanna, her parents, her illness, Alison – and Diane.

A little metal bridge spanned the river, and I'd just finished recounting my sorrowful tale to Sarah when we reached it. Sarah leaned on the bridge, and peered into the water. I stared down, too, and saw a large dragonfly fluttering around, looking just like a miniature helicopter. Sparkles of light danced on the water.

'What do you like doing?' Sarah asked, still gazing into the river.

'Don't know.'

'Must be something you like doing.'

I thought about it.

'Writing,' I said.

'What do you write?'

'I'm writing a story – a novel.'

She glanced at me, interested. 'What about?'

'Aliens.'

'Aliens.' She didn't bat an eyelid.

'From outer space.'

'Yeah.'

There was a splash! as Zero jumped into the river. I had never seen a dog swim before, and I laughed.

'Let's throw him a stick,' suggested Sarah, and we did.

We spent a long time throwing sticks for Zero. He raced across the meadow; he shot in and out of the water. When we turned to go back to the cottage, I thought it had been one of the best afternoons I had ever had – and I decided that I would like a dog of my own. As we crossed the bridge, Sarah said, 'So you believe in aliens, do you?'

'Yes,' I said, firmly. 'Do you?' I ventured.

'Sort of.'

'Sort of?'

Sarah Tanner slung her hands in her pockets, and looked at me.

'I'm one.'

'What?'

'An alien.'

My jaw dropped.

'I'm an alien, Jane, and a stranger. Just passing through.'

'Passing through?'

'Passing through.'

My mouth was still hanging open.

'You're an alien?'

'Alien and stranger in the world.' Her face was perfectly straight. 'Jane, I live in the world, but I don't belong to it. I belong to a beautiful kingdom – one that is so beautiful, you couldn't even imagine it – and I'm one of the King's daughters. See all this?' She flung her arms out to indicate everything around us, 'This is nothing compared to that beautiful kingdom.'

I closed my mouth, and just stared at her. She was making it up – I knew that. She was making up a story, but it was a better story than any I could ever write. I wanted to hear more, but she didn't speak again, except to call Zero. It was only when we had arrived back at the cottage that Sarah spoke to me.

'And I'll tell you what else,' she said. 'If you're such a good writer, you know what you should do.'

'What?'

'You should write to Heather.'

* * * * * * * *

I leaned back against my pillow, and chewed the end of my biro. My story was strewn across the bed.

Could Sandra Richmond fit a dog into her fighter? Would it have to wear a space helmet?

I was feeling sleepy. What an interesting day it had been! What a lovely walk I'd had, with Sarah and Zero. I put the biro down. I wouldn't add the paragraph about the dog. Sandra Richmond wouldn't have a dog in a fighter. I didn't want my story to be unbelievable....

My eyes snapped wide open. Sarah had said she was an alien! I smiled, and remembered what she had said about the beautiful kingdom where she belonged. She was a King's daughter! What a fantastic story that was, I thought.

I mean, she hadn't meant it, had she? It wasn't true. It was just something she was making up.

Wasn't it?

In That Beautiful Kingdom

'That's it, then. It's all arranged.'

'What's all arranged, Mum?' I asked.

Mum took a slice of toast, and began buttering it.

'I'm going to see your dad.'

'What? When?'

'I'm going up to London later on today, and I'll be back sometime tomorrow.'

'Mum, can I come?'

'No, Janie.'

'Why not?'

'You just can't.'

'But I haven't seen Dad for ages. Why can't I come?'

'Janie, please.' Mum bit into her toast. 'Dad and I have got something to sort out.'

I felt the old familiar fear start to crawl up my body.

'What are you going to sort out, Mum?'

'I'll tell you when I get back.'

My stomach churned. I felt sick. This was it, then. My parents were going to divorce.

Gran came in from the garden.

'I'm going at tea-time, Mum, and I'll be back late tomorrow. I'm sure you and Janie will have a great time together while I'm gone!'

'Oh, yes, we will – won't we, Jane?'

'Mmm,' I said. I still felt sick. I knew Mum and Dad still had problems, but it was so easy to forget them at Gran's.

'By the way, you've got to get someone out to look at your phone, or test the line, or something,' Mum was saying. 'It's still making that crackling sort of noise.'

'Yes, yes,' said Gran. 'I'll get around to it. Jane? Are you feeling all right?'

I mumbled something about wanting to go outside, and I wandered into the garden, and tried to blink back a few tears.

'Jane?'

That was Gran's kindly voice behind me. She slipped her arm round my shoulders.

'You're disappointed, aren't you, dear? Well, never mind. You'll see Dad soon enough.'

I tried to swallow, and found it hard.

'Come on, Jane. Cheer up! You had a good time yesterday, didn't you, with Sarah and Zero?'

'Yes,' I said, 'I like your friends, Gran.'

'And they like you! Poor old Mrs. Rose – she was so worried she'd frightened you with her fainting like that. She's always doing it. Makes a habit of it. And Mrs. Day said you were charming.'

I smiled a little.

'And you got on very well with Sarah, didn't you?'

I nodded.

'Yes, she's a lovely girl. Best youth leader we ever had at our church. Takes the older Bible Class pupils, you know.'

I was surprised. Sarah took Bible Class? Perhaps Bible Class wasn't quite as bad as I'd thought.

'She tells great stories,' I said.

'Oh yes! What story has she been telling you, then?'

'About being an alien.'

'About being a what?'

'An alien.'

'I'm sorry, dear. I thought you said "alien".'

'I did, Gran. Sarah said she was an alien and a stranger in the world.'

'Oh, I see!' Gran started to smile.

'She told me about this beautiful kingdom where she belongs. She said she was one of the King's daughters.' I sighed. 'I wish I could make up a story like that!'

'Oh, Sarah didn't make that story up, Jane.'

'What do you mean?'

'It's a true story.' Gran gave me a squeeze. 'Sarah's been telling you about the kingdom of God.'

I shook my head. 'No, she was talking about aliens.'

'Well, Jane, in the Bible Christians are called "aliens and strangers in the world".'

'Why are they called that?' I asked, mystified.

'Jane, if you were to go and live in a foreign land for a time, you'd be a stranger there, wouldn't you? An "alien".'

'Yes.'

'Well, Christians believe that when they decide to trust in Jesus, they become part of his kingdom – a kingdom you can't see here and now, because it's invisible. But even though they can't see it with their eyes, Christians know they belong to it, so they are "aliens and strangers" in the world you *can* see. They are God's children, children of the King, learning more about Jesus every day, and living for him, until the time comes when they go to be with Jesus, and live with him for ever in that beautiful kingdom.'

Gran looked at me as if she expected me to ask some questions, but I was taking it all in. We stood there together, listening to the twittering birds, and by the time I had thought of a question or two, Mum was approaching us, her brow very furrowed – she looked worried.

'Janie, are you OK? I'm sorry I can't take you to London with me.'

'It's all right, Mum.' I smiled at her. 'I'm going to write a letter.' And I darted indoors.

* * * * * * * *

'Oh dear,' said Gran, replacing the receiver, 'That really was a bad line. I must get something done about it.'

I had my head in a cupboard full of clutter, and I hadn't really heard much of the conversation Gran had been having on the phone. It was Mum. I'd spoken with her. She seemed very distant and crackly, but that was Gran's phone. Gran's ears were more used to the crackling, so I had quickly handed the receiver over to her.

'Oh dear,' said Gran, again. 'Bad news, Jane.'

'What is it, Gran?' I said, with an inward groan.

'Your mum won't be coming back today, after all. She's not coming back till Friday.'

'Oh.'

Gran grunted as she got down on her knees beside me.

'You haven't cleaned these cupboards out for years, have you!' I said, and she shook her head, and started looking at some of the old magazines and books I had pulled out.

'Oh, look at this, Jane. A photo of your grandad, it just fell out of this book.'

I looked at the old photo. I'd never known Grandad. In this picture he looked quite young, holding the bridle of a pony. A young girl was sitting on the pony.

'That's your mum!' said Gran.

I was gazing at the photograph, when Gran picked up another book.

'Oh, this isn't mine. This belongs to the church. I'll let Sarah have this when she comes round later.'

'Sarah's coming?' I said, 'Sarah Tanner?'

'Yes. She's popping round later to collect some song-books. Now, where *are* the song-books? That's the question.'

I carried on clearing out the cupboard, feeling very happy at the thought of a visit from my new-found friend.

There were only a couple of books left in the

cupboard. They smelled very musty, and I looked at the covers. One was a thick, grey book called, *Doctrines*. I put that down. And then I gasped in amazement, as my eyes rested on a very familiar book indeed.

'Gran! This is *my* book.' I leafed through the pages. 'It's the book you bought me, years and years ago.' Yes, it was another copy of my little Jesus book.

'So it is!' Gran peeped over my shoulder. 'You haven't still got that little book, have you, Jane?'

'Yes, I have. It's upstairs. I brought it with me.'

'Did you really?'

'Yes.' I read from the page in front of me. 'Look, Gran. *"Your Father has been pleased to give you the kingdom"*. That must be the same kingdom you were talking about yesterday.'

Gran took the book from me, and smiled down at the text.

'My book's in better condition, though,' I said.

She laughed. 'I'm surprised you still read that old book, Jane – surprised, but very pleased.'

'I know it's a kid's book, Gran. But – ' I hesitated. If I told Gran that I had started to pray to God, she might ask why, and I really didn't want to talk about Mum and Dad. The word 'divorce' stuck in my throat. I didn't even want to think about it until I had to. Secretly, I was relieved that Mum wouldn't be back till Friday. At least I had a few more days before I had to face up to any real unpleasantness. Still, I thought, glumly, I suppose I will have to face it. I supposed I would live with Mum. Would Dad get an Alison? Did he already have one? Would I have to meet her?

'Jane? Jane, did you hear me? Are you dreaming again?'

'Oh. What, Gran? Oh – sorry.'

'I said, do you ever talk to God?'

I decided to be honest, now that she had asked me directly.

'Yes. But – '

'But what?'

'I know he's there, Gran, and I know he hears me. But he's not very quick at replying sometimes, is he?'

Gran was taken aback.

'Er – no. But sometimes he wants us to wait, and to trust him. It's called being patient.'

'I'm no good at that.'

'Not many people are!'

'Still, he's not as fast at answering as I thought he might be – at least, on some things.'

Gran seemed to think this very funny.

'Besides,' I added, dolefully, 'Every time I think about God, I seem to see Jesus.'

Gran caught my hand. 'Then God is answering you!'

'What?'

'He's pointing you to his Son, Jesus.'

'Why would he want to do that?'

'Because our relationship with God starts with Jesus.' Gran looked thoughtful. 'Drains!' she exclaimed.

'Drains?' I said, blankly.

'Drains, Jane. When you've got a blocked drain, you need someone to clear out all the muck and rubbish and horrible stuff, don't you?'

'I suppose so.'

'It's the same with us and God,' Gran nodded, with a twinkle in her eye. 'You see, Jane, all the wrong things we do in our lives have blocked up and messed up and ruined our friendship with God. But God still loves us, and he worked out a plan to put things right between us and him.'

'How did he do that?'

'He sent his Son, Jesus. When Jesus died on the cross, he took all the punishment we deserve for all the wrong things we've done – the things that have blocked up and ruined our friendship with God.'

I sat back, impressed.

'So you see, Jane, to have a friendship with God, here and now and for ever, we must trust in Jesus and what he did for us when he died. He rose from the dead, you know, and he's alive, even though we can't see him.'

In my mind, I suddenly saw that stained glass window of Jesus carrying a lamb. What were the words written beneath his feet? I remembered.

'Come unto me.'

'That's it, Jane.' Gran smiled. 'I'll tell you what, it's a long time since I came to Jesus! You know, I always thought I was a Christian because I used to go to church and I did so try to be a good person! But it's jolly hard work trying to be good and I soon found out that I couldn't keep it up, and anyway, the good things I did would never cancel out the bad! So one day, I turned round to God and said, "I can't do it. I can't make myself good enough to please you!" and do you know what God said to me? "Well, I'm glad you realise it at last! Now let me help you!" and I just gave my life completely to Jesus, and he gave me his Spirit so that I could start to live a good life in his strength – not mine!'

'Gran...' I took a deep breath. 'Gran, I want to give my

life to Jesus, just like you did.' And I suddenly knew that I wanted this more than anything else in the whole world.

Gran grasped my hand. 'Would you like me to pray with you, dear? Or would you rather be on your own?'

'No, please stay, Gran.' I wanted her to be there, just in case I did something wrong. I really wanted Jesus in my life. I wasn't going to miss out just because I said the wrong words or something! But as it happened, the words just seemed to flow naturally, as we both knelt there in Gran's cluttered room.

'Hello, Jesus,' I said, 'I've heard what you did for me when you died on the cross. I believe it and I believe you're alive right now even though I can't see you. Please forgive me for all the things I've done wrong. Help me to follow you. Come into my life and help me live for you – just like you did with Gran.'

It had started out as a whisper – but by the end of my prayer my voice was loud and confident. There were tears on Gran's cheeks, and on mine, but we were both laughing. I'd never felt such happiness before. It was as if someone had filled up my chest with joy.

'Oh, Gran!' I said, hugging her. 'Oh, Gran!'

* * * * * * * *

'Sarah! Sarah! Great news!'

I grabbed her by the hand, and she almost fell in the door.

'Sarah, I'm an alien.'

'Yeah?'

'I'm an alien and a stranger in the world, just like you. *I'm* in that beautiful kingdom you were talking about! I'm one of the King's daughters, now – I am, you know, because I asked Jesus to come into my life.'

I felt Gran's hand on my shoulder. She was nodding at Sarah, and she looked too happy to speak.

'That's great!' cried Sarah. 'It's great, isn't it, Zero?'

He jumped around us, barking because we were so excited.

'You know, angels are dancing around in heaven because of this!' Sarah told me.

'Angels? I thought they sat on Christmas trees.'

'Um... no, Jane.'

'Oh, and Sarah – I wrote that letter.'

'Great!'

'Shall we have a cup of tea to celebrate?' said Gran.

'Tea? No! This calls for ice cream!' said Sarah, 'That's if it's not too near to your dinner – '

'No! Go on. Ice cream sounds lovely,' said Gran.

'OK. Come on, Jane. We'll nip down to the village shop. I'll treat us all to ice creams.'

Sarah marched off down the path, and Zero and I bounced along behind her. Zero didn't bounce so much when Sarah slipped a rope lead over his head.

As we bounded along, I told Sarah everything Gran had explained to me about Jesus. I don't think Sarah Tanner got a word in at all until we reached the shop, where she handed me Zero's lead and asked me to hold on to him while she bought the ices. Then she went inside. Just before Sarah came out again, a family group of a man, a woman, and a little girl of about nine came strolling by. The little girl came over and stroked Zero's head, and the adults laughed before they all disappeared into the shop. I remembered that Mum and Dad were 'sorting out' their problems.

'Hello?' said Sarah's voice. 'Are you with us, Jane?'

'Oh! Sorry. I was just thinking.'

She was smiling at me, ice creams clutched in both hands.

'Sarah, can I ask you something?'

'Sure. Fire away.'

'Now that I'm a Christian, will God give me what I want?'

'Hey! We pray "*your* will be done, Lord!" you know! And sometimes God's will isn't our will. Think about it.'

I decided to be frank.

'I think my parents are getting divorced.'

Sarah seemed surprised.

'Will God make them stay together?'

Sarah sat down on a low wall beside a rubbish bin, and motioned for me to sit beside her.

'Listen, Jane. People don't always live like God wants them to. Sometimes they think their own way of doing things is best – not God's way. And he won't force them to go his way.'

'Oh.' I gazed forlornly at Zero.

'Come on,' said Sarah, 'let's pray.'

'What – here?'

'Yeah. Why not?'

Empty Coke cans, ice cream wrappers and wasps didn't seem the right setting, somehow, to pray to God. But Sarah had her eyes shut, so I shut mine, too.

'Dear Lord Jesus,' said Sarah, 'you know everything. You know all about Jane's mum and dad, and you also know that she loves them both, and doesn't want them to split up. It would be great, Lord, if they could stay together and be happy.' She was quiet for a moment, and then went on. 'And Lord, please give Jane your peace in her heart. Help her to know that now she has decided to trust in you, she need never be afraid again, because you'll always be there for her, whatever happens, now and for ever.'

I stared at her in awe. How did she know I'd been so afraid? She was grinning at me as she handed me an ice cream.

'You'll never be alone again, Jane. Jesus will never ever leave you.'

She unwrapped another ice, and gave it to Zero.

We didn't talk much on the way home. My mind was racing with new thoughts, and I whispered a silent prayer in my mind.

'Hello, God. What a wonderful day it's been. I do hope my parents won't get divorced. It'll be horrible if they do. But I know you'll help me be strong if the worst happens.' And then I added, 'Oh, but Jesus, please, please, please don't let the worst happen!'

The New Future

It was the best letter I had ever received in my life. I held it tightly, and read it again. I especially liked the last bit.

'I don't know why Olivia Gates signed "your best friend, Olivia" on my card. You're my best friend, Jane.'

Good old Heather! She was feeling better, and had replied to my letter by return of post. I was so glad that I'd written to her.

'Jane!'

'Coming, Mum.'

I put the letter down, and felt a twinge of sickness. I was nervous. I knew as soon as I went downstairs, I would find out if my parents were going to divorce. There were what felt like marbles in my stomach. But I wasn't afraid. No. I was part of God's kingdom, now. I belonged to Jesus, and I had to trust him – whatever happened.

Mum was in the living room, relaxing in a comfortable chair. She looked less tired than when she had arrived, half an hour ago. One of Gran's cups of tea had perked her up, but she still had dark shadows under her eyes.

'Do you know,' she said, 'I've taken so many taxis, buses and trains lately, I can't quite believe that I've stopped at last. I half expect this chair to zoom off up the lane. Oh, it's busy in London. I don't think I'd like to live there.'

I perched on the arm of her chair.

'Gran says you've been very good while I've been away.'

'Of course!' I said.

'Gran says you've done something special, Janie.'

'I've given my life to Jesus!' I said.

'I've been doing some praying myself, recently.'

'That's what started me off!' I said, excitedly. 'Did you know, Mum, I'm a King's daughter, now? I – '

Mum coughed. She wasn't a King's daughter – well, not yet. I decided to explain it all to her some other time, when she wasn't so tired.

'I'll go and do the washing up,' said Gran, 'leave you two to talk.'

Gran left the room, and we could hear her clattering cups and saucers about in the kitchen.

'Janie,' said Mum, 'I've got something to tell you.'

Here it comes, I thought. Jesus – help!

'Dad and I have decided – '

'You're getting a divorce.'

'What? No! Janie – of course not! Where on earth did you get that idea?'

'You're not? You're not getting a divorce?'

'No. Janie! How could you think – '

I suddenly hugged her and hugged her, overjoyed.

'He's done it, Mum! He's done it! He's answered my prayer!'

'But Janie – '

'Oh, Mum. I'm so happy!'   .

'Good. But Janie, there *is* something I want to tell you.'

I stopped hugging her, and sat back.

'What is it, then, Mum?'

'Janie, I don't know how you're going to take this. Oh dear. Janie, I'm sorry, but we're going to have to move house – away from all your friends. You'll have to go to a different school.'

I couldn't believe what I was hearing.

'It's been very hard for your dad just lately. He's been so busy, working longer hours than usual, because his boss has been in hospital, and that's meant extra pressure for Dad. But even when his boss is back at work, it's not really convenient for Dad to keep working in London and then having to travel all the way home to Gipley. He's pretty fed up with living in digs through the week. He's had enough of it, and so have I.'

'Oh!' I said.

'Anyway, we didn't know what to do, because we knew that if we moved nearer to London, it would mean you would have to leave St. Catherine's – and it's such a good school.' Mum's eyes searched my face. 'But after your latest report – and let's be honest, your other reports haven't been so wonderful, either, have they – well, we thought a fresh start might be a good thing for all three of us.'

'But where will we live?'

'We're thinking of a little town not far from the motorway – about half an hour from Tamsford.'

'Gran! Did you hear that! Gran!'

I started to do a little dance round the room.

'Wow! Oh wow!'

Gran appeared in the kitchen doorway, and laughed.

'Wow!' I said. 'Wow! Wow! Wow!'

* * * * * * * *

I stared out of the window. Blinking up at the black sky, dotted with twinkling stars, I sighed with happiness, and forgot about the people in the cottage opposite.

'God. Oh God! Oh, thank you, God. I do like trusting in your Son, Jesus. He's great.'

I rested my elbows on the windowsill.

'You've done more than I even asked you for, because I'm going to get away from St. Catherine's for ever.'

I sighed again.

'Mind you, I'm not getting out of it that easily. Mum says it takes time to sell a house, so I'll have to go back there for a bit. I'll have to trust you to help me. But it doesn't seem so bad, now that I know you're going to be there with me every day.'

I thought about the letter.

'I'm going to tell Heather all about you. I think it's too late for her mum and dad to get together again, but I don't know. Still, it's not too late for Heather to get to know you, though, and then she won't have to be scared, she can feel all peaceful about things, like I do. And perhaps Diane will believe in you, too, and then she won't be so horrible. Perhaps even Olivia Gates will come to know you, and then you can do something about her being so smug.'

I was so happy! I would see more of Dad, and more of Gran, in the future. I'd be able to stay friends with Sarah Tanner. She had already promised to write to me when I went back home, but it was wonderful to think that there would be plenty more walks with her and Zero. The future looked bright.

We were staying an extra week at Gran's, then Dad was going to pick us up and take us home. I had already decided to go to church with Gran, and Mum had said she would come, too. I was looking forward to Sunday.

'I might even go to Bible Class,' I mused, 'Gran says it's not compulsory, and there are people my age in Sarah's class.'

Gazing into the sky, I thought how beautiful it was. I knew now there were thousands of God's angels flapping about out there, unseen. Sarah had told me something about angels, and how they protect God's people. I smiled. Aliens of any description couldn't get me now!

I flopped into bed. I got out again, because I'd sat on a load of paper. It was my story.

I put the pages back into my suitcase, and laughed out loud. 'Aliens!' I said.

Sandra Richmond climbed out of her battle-scarred fighter.

'Well, Sandra,' said Paul Sinclaire, looking at her with admiration, 'you're free, and the aliens are all defeated.'

'Yep!' said Sandra, slinging her hands into her pockets.

'So, what're you going to do next?'

'I'm going to do something really challenging, for a change.'

'What?' asked Paul, interested. 'Deep space? Time travel? What are you going to do, Sandra?'

Colonel Sandra Richmond reached into her fighter, and brought out a Bible.

'I'm going to tell the world about Jesus.'

Sheila Jacobs Books

Life with Jane Series

Aliens and Strangers 1-85792-2794
Rollercoaster Time 1-85792-3855
Something to Shout About 1-85792-4886

Life with Sammy Series

A Different Life 1-85792-5904
This New Life 1-85792-6617
A Life Worth Living 1-85792-7303
It's My Life 1-85792-8350

A Life Worth Living

Saying no to Sex •
Beating the Bully •
Shella Jacobs

LIGHT KEEPERS

Ten Boys who changed the World

Irene Howat

Would you like to change your world? These ten boys grew up to do just that: *Billy Graham, Brother Andrew, John Newton, George Müller, Nicky Cruz, William Carey, David Livingstone, Adoniram Judson, Eric Liddell and Luis Palau.*

Find out how Eric won the race and honoured God; David became an explorer and explained the Bible; Nicky joined the gangs and then the church; Andrew smuggled Bibles into Russia and brought hope to thousands, and John captured slaves but God used him to set them free.

Find out what God wants you to do.

ISBN: 1-85792-579-3

LIGHT KEEPERS

Ten Girls who changed the World

Irene Howat

Would you like to change your world? These ten girls grew up to do just that: **Isobel Kuhn, Helen Keller, Amy Carmichael, Gladys Aylward, Mary Slessor, Catherine Booth, Jackie Pullinger, Evelyn Brand, Joni Eareckson Tada and Corrie Ten Boom.**

Find out how Corrie saved lives; Mary saved babies; Gladys rescued 100 children; Joni survived a crippling accident and still thanked Jesus; Amy rescued orphans and never gave up; Isobel taught the Lisu about Christ; Evelyn obeyed God in India; Jackie showed love in awful conditions in Hong Kong; Helen showed determination and discovered God and Catherine rolled up her sleeves and helped the homeless!

Find out what God wants you to do.

ISBN: 1-85792-649-8